No Room for Fear

Melissa Steeves

God Bless
Melissa Steeves
1 John 4:18

XULON PRESS

CHAPTER ONE

Sydney Gillman stood beside the window of the Hope
Christian Church staring at the grey, overcast sky thinking that even the weather was a reflection of her heart. Soon
she would be asked to follow three caskets down the aisle to
the front of the church. It would be there that her husband
Grant would take her hand and they would say good-bye to
their three precious children. Sydney turned from the
window feeling like this should all be a dream but the
weight in her heart told her that this had to be real. *How
would she go on?*

The funeral director came to the door and asked that the
family get ready to enter the church sanctuary. Sydney
looked at him and, for the life of her, she could not remember his name. Funny she had met with him at least a dozen
times in the last few days and yet he seemed like a stranger
to her now. Looking around the room Sydney saw all of her
and Grant's families were present. Each wore a mask of
grief and sought one another for comfort. Slowly Grant
walked to her side and took her hand. Not knowing what to
say, she let him lead her slowly down the aisle behind three
caskets as their families followed. As they neared the front

Sydney noticed all the flowers and wreaths that lined the front of the church—each one expressing sympathy for the loss of nephew, niece, grandson, granddaughter, son, and daughter. All of the pews were lined with family and friends watching this sad processional. *Why three caskets, God? Why three? Couldn't it have been one or two or, better yet, none?* No, Sydney stood here watching three caskets, the exact number of children she had given birth to. Sydney's chest tightened as the first casket adorned with red roses and a red baseball jersey bearing the number seven rolled into place. Brendan, her tall, strong sixteen-year-old. So much life left to live and yet it was cut short...too short. He loved baseball and she had been his biggest fan. Brendan had just finished pitching his first year for the Spring Hills High School Cardinals. Sydney, proud mom that she was, had been at every game. Except for the blonde hair and green eyes that Brendan had inherited from Sydney, he was the spitting image of his father. Tall with an athletic build, girls were always trying to get his attention and little children followed him everywhere. At church Brendan always had one of the little ones on his knee. Kids loved Brendan because they knew that he loved them and would always have time for them. *Brendan...why God why?*

The second casket, laden with white roses and a well-worn navy ball cap with the space needle embroidered on the front, caught her eye. Scott, her little Scotty had already turned fourteen. Scotty had worn that ball cap all the time to hide his unruly brown hair. Always too busy to comb his hair, on went the ball cap. Sydney had bought the cap for him in Seattle while attending a woman's conference. Scotty had been so excited that it became a permanent part of his wardrobe. Brown hair and blue eyes like his dad but smaller and stockier than Brendan, Scotty was more like Sydney in character—quiet, and with a great sense of humor. Scotty loved practical jokes and Sydney was usually the target. How he had loved to sneak up and scare her to death. Computers had been Scotty's passion and he had always fixed her errors with a smile, saying, "Mom, you are hopeless with the computer and one day, when I take over Microsoft, I am going to create a program just for you. I'll call it Sydneyware it will be the ultimate in computers for dummies software." *Oh, Scotty...why God, why?*

The final casket covered in pale pink roses and the small white teddy bear with the frayed right ear was wheeled alongside of the other two. It was so small. Sarah Rose...she loved the sound of both names together and insisted everyone use both names when addressing her. Sarah Rose was only six, just starting her life. Her brothers had adored their little sister and carried her around on their backs and shoulders all the time. Sarah Rose was just about three when she finally walked because they had always insisted on carrying her. Sydney always suspected Sarah Rose walked before that but only when no one was around or looking. Sarah Rose had been a sweet surprise for Sydney and Grant when they thought that their family was complete with two active boys. *Please, God, not Sarah Rose.* Her blonde ringlets and big blue eyes could talk her daddy into just about anything. *Why?* Her sweet smile and singsong voice was gone forever. She was only six. *The casket is too small, surely this can't be happening.*

No, not all three. Grant, how will we survive? Sydney just couldn't go on, the pain was just too much for her to bear. Sydney's heart was beating way too fast when surely it shouldn't be beating at all for all the pieces it was broken into. *Why God? Why did you do this?* Things had been so good; a great marriage, three beautiful children. She had known this would happen. God was out to punish her because it was so good. *Why, why did you do this God?* Sydney's heart was breaking again into yet another million pieces, her chest growing heavier as each breath became harder and harder to draw. *Just keep walking; make it to the front pew before you collapse.* Left, right, left—suddenly she couldn't breathe at all and everything started to slowly go black. Reaching out for anyone or anything she cried, "Grant...Grant, help me. I can't breathe...help me, please... Grant... Grant...."

"Sydney...honey...you're shaking like a leaf. Are you okay, Sydney...Syd, are you okay? Syd, wake up honey—it was just a dream". Grant had awakened to Sydney's pleas for help and could see her reaching out, trying desperately to grab for him. Grant grasped her hands and gently shook her, trying to wake her from the nightmare.

"Sydney...honey...you're shaking like a leaf, are you okay?"

As the darkness lifted from her mind, Sydney realized that while it had only been a dream, she still harboured a deep dread that it could happen. God was waiting to punish her and take her through some trials because her life was too good; Christians needed trials to be good Christians, right? That's what she had always been taught.

"Okay. . .now, just hold me, Grant, please? Just hold me." Sydney felt weak and exhausted; the growing fear and the wait for the inevitable to happen was taking its toll on her.

"Syd, do you want to tell me about it? By your reactions this dream was worse than any you have had before. I don't know what's haunting your dreams but it sure has you scared. Tell me Syd, I want to help." Grant was deeply concerned. He knew that Sydney had been struggling with something. He had been waking her from nightmares for more than a year now, but her reply was always the same.

"O, Grant, its just one of those falling dreams and they just seem so real. I'll be okay. Just hold me."

"Okay Syd, but you know from this end it seems like something more. Do you think we should pray about it?" Grant loved her dearly and wanted to help her fight this struggle if only she would let him. His only recourse had been to pray because, ultimately, God would be the only one who could help her, especially if she pushed her own husband away.

"Sure, but you pray, I'm just too tired to think straight." As Sydney spoke the words she felt like she was really just too exhausted to do anything. Her burden was weighing down every part of her and she wouldn't be rid of it until God had finished with His vengeance. Even then, she knew the grief would be more than she could bear. But the waiting would be over and it was the waiting that was killing her. The fear was overwhelming. She felt she must be going mad, but she couldn't tell anybody for fear she might be committed just like... *No, she mustn't think about things like that. Grant was so strong and she loved him more than life itself. His own trust and dependence on God were admirable, but she just couldn't understand why it was that he never worried about all the terrible things that she was sure were coming.*

As Grant prayed, Sydney felt herself relax, his voice could always soothe her; she was drifting, and soon sleep would take over. Sweet sleep, where hopefully peace would reign until morning and there would be no more nightmares, at least for this night. Tomorrow was another day. Another day to wait really. She must think of something to do to get her mind off this waiting for at least a few hours. *What could she do? Yes, Maria—she would go to see Maria. Maybe spend some time in Maria's rose garden, a place that always seemed to refresh her soul.* Maria would offer her comfort without having to know what the problem was. Sydney had known Maria for what seemed like a lifetime. They had both grown up in Tilson, a small town north of Spring Hills, where both of their families had farmed. The families had spent every Sunday afternoon together after church and had also vacationed with one another every year.

Although there was ten years difference between their ages, Maria and Sydney were like sisters. Their relationship had only grown stronger when Maria had married her high school sweetheart and moved to Spring Hills. Sydney had followed after finishing her own schooling and had lived with Maria and Barry while she tried to decide what to do next with her life.

Yes, that is what she would do. Tomorrow she would see Maria and avoid the waiting if only for an hour or two. Yes, that was it. She would go see Maria and her rose garden where they would sit in the sunlight, sipping tea. With this one small hope Sydney could now fall asleep. Shifting slightly in Grant's arms, Sydney gave way to what she hoped would be a peaceful sleep.

CHAPTER TWO

Sydney woke with a start, the house was too quiet, and Grant's side of the bed was empty. She listened to hear if the shower was running but silence was the only reply. Sydney leaned over to grab the big navy blue terry bathrobe from the chair by the bed when she noticed the clock said nine o'clock. *It couldn't be, the alarm was set for six-thirty, and no one could sleep through that alarm. Brendan even complained he could hear it downstairs. Heaven forbid that Brendan be woken up one minute before the absolute last minute.* Coffee. She could smell coffee and the aroma drew her out of bed and down the hall. *It must be the coffee she had just purchased at the new coffee place downtown...what was it called? Oh, yes the Coffee Nook.* The coffee's aroma lifted the last remnants of sleep from her mind. As Sydney walked down the hall she checked Scott and Sarah Rose's rooms to find the beds made. *Now that's odd,* she thought, *they never make their beds unless there is a threat of punishment.* Walking into the kitchen another oddity struck her—it was clean, and the dishwasher was running.

"I'm starting to feel like I'm in an episode of the Twilight Zone...oh great, now I'm talking to myself. What next?" Sydney reached for her favorite mug on a hook right beside the coffeepot. Filling it with the aromatic dark liquid she checked the kitchen clock—it too said 9:05 am. Sydney found it odd she could sleep through the alarm clock and the noise from early morning family rituals, of which she was sure the neighbors heard every morning. Passing the fridge a note caught her eye. Grabbing it, Sydney proceeded across the dining room to her favorite chair next to the large bay window in the living room. The remote for the stereo was on the small coffee table; she leaned over and hit play. Michael W Smith filled the room as she dropped into the chair. Big, red, and well worn, it was where she could get comfy and relax. Pulling the coaster closer and setting down the coffee, she read the note.

Dear Syd,

Thought you could use the extra sleep so I shut off the alarm and told the kids if they woke you I would have a whole weekend of chores for them. Sarah Rose talked her brothers into the bed-making saying it would make you feel better. I did the dishes, aren't you impressed? (It wasn't hard but I will deny that if asked) I'll pick up pizza for supper and will also pick up Brendan from ball and the other two from music lessons.

Enjoy your day, get some rest. I have an office day planned so don't bother coming to work. I got you covered, honey. Go see Maria and have coffee and don't forget your retreat meeting at 10:30. I love you and miss you already.

Hugs and kisses,
yours Forever,
Grant
xo xo xo

Grant. How had she been so lucky to find and marry this wonderful man? Many of the women Sydney talked to wondered where she had found such a sensitive, loving, helpful and handsome man. She had to admit to being amazed and wondering the same thing everyday. It's hard to believe that they had been married seventeen years. Grant's beautiful blue eyes still captivated her and her heart still fluttered whenever he walked into the room. It felt like just yesterday that she first met Grant Gillman.

When Sydney had moved in with Maria and Barry after graduation she had no plans for marriage or boyfriends until she had decided what to do with her life. Barry was the basketball coach for the Spring Hills College Bulls. They had four beautiful children—Jesse, Philip, Patrick and Glenda. Sydney lived in the partially finished basement and soon had made her room feel like home. A few posters of exotic beaches with blue water and white sand, a stereo, book collection and her big burgundy quilt that Grandma Ruth had made. The blanket brought back all kinds of memories and when she was snuggled beneath it she felt close to Grandma.

Sydney had found a job just a few days after arriving in town. Pet Haven was the ideal job. She loved handling the animals and had no fear of them after being raised with all sorts of farm animals. Besides, she got every weekend off. The pay wasn't bad and it gave her a lot of time to read books. Sydney loved to read and the stories always took her far away to distant lands and times. Maria always teased Sydney that she spent way too much time with her nose in a book.

About three months after moving to Spring Hills, Sydney came home from work on a Friday evening to find Maria standing at the back door waiting. Maria's short black hair was hidden beneath her red Bulls ball cap and she was wearing a new navy Bulls golf shirt with jeans. Maria's shirts were always untucked because she felt it hid the tummy left behind after four children. Maria wore black trendy glasses so that she could see the roses with style, as she put it. A large "Go Bulls Go" sign completed the outfit.

"I have a babysitter and it's ladies night out. How does foot longs and Coke at a basketball game sound?"

"Well, I suppose I could come. What team will Barry's team annihilate tonight?" Sydney enjoyed watching basketball, and so far this season, Barry's team had been undefeated. Besides, it was Friday and she didn't want to sit at home by herself.

"It's the state champs Brooksville Buffalos and I may have to get a little loud—you know, to encourage the guys." Maria was Barry and his team's biggest fan. In fact, the team always came to their house for homemade pizza the night before big games. Sydney always stayed late at the Living Room Coffeehouse reading her latest book in order to avoid all the guys when they came over.

"Maria, when aren't you loud and encouraging at a game?"

"Well I'm in especially if its ladies night. Foot longs and coke is on me because today was payday."

"You're on and you know me, I'll never turn down free food. Let's roll'"

"I just need to change. I'll be right back." Sydney was already halfway down the stairs. As she entered her room, there was Mr. Teddy on the floor. Glenda must have been in here trying to have tea with Sydney's stuffed animals again.

Grabbing the bear, she threw it on the bed. Going to her closet, she grabbed an old pair of denim jeans and the Bull's sweatshirt that Maria had given her as a moving in, welcome to Spring Hills gift. Maria had insisted that everyone in the house had to have one piece of Bull's attire just in case they needed to wear it sometime. Maria would be proud tonight, especially when it was such an important game. Slipping runners on her feet and grabbing a clip, she ran up the stairs struggling to put up her shoulder length curly blonde hair. She wished for straight hair because all the styles nowadays were for straight hair. Oh well, the curls were just to hard to tame, so she kept it longer so it was easy put it up. It offered some semblance of control when she put it up.

Maria was already in the van with it running and she was revving the engine to let Sydney know that she was trying to act impatient. Sydney grabbed the much too large purse and headed out the front door, wishing the babysitter good luck. She really didn't need luck because Maria's four kids were really well behaved.

"Syd, I have never understood why you carry such a big purse. Doesn't it get heavy?" Shaking her head, Maria backed out the driveway and headed to the college, which was only about five blocks away.

"Maria, I have important things in here. Besides, I need something that will fit whatever book I may be reading at the time and a bottle of water. Oh course I can't leave my favorite stainless steel coffee mug, just in case I ever pass a coffee shop." Sydney laughed, realizing how ridiculous it sounded but she just found it easier to carry a bag big enough than be juggling everything back and forth to work. "Besides, I'm building muscle. You should try it, it does wonders for the arms."

"Sorry, Syd, but I carried a diaper bag for eight years and I am really enjoying a small compact wallet on a string. I also built muscle carrying around four kids. Oh look, a parking spot right near Barry's car. What luck…you'd think I had called ahead or something." As Maria pulled into the parking space by Barry's VW, Sydney noticed how full the parking lot was.

"Looks like Barry will have a full house to witness the outcome of this game. Are the Buffalos that good?" Sydney opened the door and jumped out before Maria had even turned the van off.

"Yes, the Buffalos are that good. Barry has been working hard with the team all week in preparation for this game. I think he's a little nervous. He left earlier than usual so he could pray with Pastor Steve."

Pastor Steve Ironside was the pastor of Hope Christian Church. The congregation was between 100-150 of which Maria and Barry were a part. Sydney went most Sundays with the Bennett's and was impressed by the warmth and caring that was shown to her.

"So, will Pastor Steve be here then?" Syd liked him well enough but didn't want to give him the opportunity to hound her to get more involved and attend more regularly. If Sydney had taken the time to get to know him, she would have known that Pastor Steve never would have done that, but as she did with all other pastors, Syd kept them at arm's length.

"Yes, Pastor Steve will be here. He is a huge basketball fan. Barry and Steve could talk about the game for hours." Maria led the way in to the college gym and Sydney noticed that the game was ready to start. Maria's two seats behind the bench were empty because every one knew that they were for the coach's wife. Sydney spotted Barry right about the same time that he spotted Maria. Barry was not much taller than Maria and was carrying some extra weight that he contributed to Maria's great cooking. He had dark brown hair and a bushy mustache to match. Barry smiled and winked at Maria and Sydney knew as soon as there was time he would be over to see her. Sydney admired their marriage, their love being evident to all who knew them, and they always found time to spend alone together. Someday Sydney hoped for a love like that for herself.

"So, should I go for the food now or wait until later? Just so you know, I'm famished and I think that I might have to get some kind of chocolate thing for dessert."

"You're always hungry, especially when chocolate is involved. What is it with you and chocolate? I'm starting to think that you could live strictly on coffee and chocolate." Maria loved to tease Sydney about her love of chocolate, especially with a good cup of coffee.

"Well, I'm sure there will be some kind of study to say that chocolate is good for you so I'm just getting a head start on healthy eating. So how about the food, shall I go now?"

"Actually, I am kind of hungry myself. Better go get that food so we can keep up our strength for cheering." With that Maria's attention was drawn back to the pre-game activities on the court.

The game was just underway as Sydney stood to go and get the munchies. Sydney lifted her purse and gave it a little swing on to her shoulder when to her horror it connected with something solid. Turning slowly to see what the purse had hit, she was horrified to see one of the basketball players holding his head as he rose to face the person who had hit him in the head. Now Sydney was wishing the floor would open up and swallow her—especially before he realized who it was that had hit him. It was then that Sydney saw the big deep blue eyes. She also noticed the tall six-foot athletic build compared to her five foot five and three-quarters. He was tall dark and handsome...and those eyes! She could definitely get lost in those eyes. Sydney's heart raced as she was held in his gaze, wondering at how this one man could evoke such a response in her.

"Excuse me, Miss, Grant Gillman's the name and may I apologize for my big head getting in the way?" Grant smiled and was immediately intrigued with this blonde cutie with green eyes. The blonde curls were swept up but a few had escaped and were framing her oval face in a way that made him want to reach over and gently brush them to the side. Grant definitely wanted to know this girl better. Grant smiled and with a chuckle in his voice said "Would you like me to help you to the exit with that purse? It seems mighty heavy for such a lovely lady."

"Um...oh...I'm...sorry...you...what? This old thing isn't that big...you should see the purse I shop with." As Grant laughed she knew that this man was someone to get to know better. "I'm Sydney Forrester and I'm here with my friend Maria Bennett. Her husband is..."

"Coach Barry, yea I know him. Hi Maria, and thanks for the leftovers. I haven't eaten that well since I was home the last time. Well, if you don't need any help, I better get back to the game at hand. Nice to meet you, Sydney Forrester. I hope that I'll see you again."

He smiled and started to turn, then looked back at her deep into her eyes and said "Soon. I want to see you again very soon."

Then Grant Gillman was gone as Barry called for him. Sydney shook herself back to reality and headed out to get the food quickly before Maria could say anything. Never had a man had that much affect on Sydney and she wasn't ready to talk about it with anyone...not yet anyway.

With foot longs and Coke in hand and two milk chocolate and almond chocolate bars in her purse Sydney headed back to the seats. Maria was standing and yelling at one of the other team's players, so Sydney was able to slip back into the seats with little said about her encounter with Grant. Sydney settled in to watch the game and couldn't help but watch Grant the entire time.

She was jolted back to reality when Maria leaned over and nudged her. "You're hooked."

Caught off-guard, Sydney stuttered, "No. No, I'm not...what are you talking about?" Sydney was surprised that the game was already over. Somehow it had slipped by while she was, well, daydreaming?

"You know, Grant. You haven't taken your eyes off him since you beat him up in the first half." Maria chuckled and waved at Barry as he walked across the court towards her. Sydney was a little unsettled that she was so readable but then again Maria had known her for a long time. Sydney did appreciate the fact that Maria had not said anything until after the game was over and now she just had to keep her from saying anything to Barry. Sydney was sure it was Barry's life mission to tease her and this would give Barry way too much ammunition.

"Maria..."

"Hey Barry, Sydney is going to love coming to all the games for the rest of the season." Too late. Sydney was now looking for all exits and which one would be closest because she knew what was coming.

"Why, she just loves to watch my amazing coaching talent?" Barry was enjoying seeing Sydney squirm and knowing the real reason from talk in the locker room. He couldn't pass up this opportunity that had been just dropped into his lap.

"No. That's why I'm here, to cheer on your amazing coaching but Sydney, well, she seems to have taken to hitting on one of your players." Maria's grin showed that she was enjoying this and was making up for being silent during the game. "I mean, she was really hitting on this guy!"

"I was not hitting on him! I mean, I hit him—accidentally—with my purse. I wasn't trying to get his attention. It was just an accident. This is hopeless, isn't it? Trying to explain?" It was then that Sydney noticed Barry laughing so hard that he was bent over.

"You know, don't you? Who told you, Barry? How did you find out? Now I'm really embarrassed. Does the whole school know?" Sydney was now wishing that the floor would open up and swallow her. This had to be worse than when she had hit Grant.

"Yes I know, and no, the whole school doesn't know—not yet, anyway. Seems one of my players has quite a large bump on the side of his head. When I asked him why he wasn't concentrating on the game he said he had a headache and was hoping to get some personal TLC from an angel in the stands carrying a large black purse with rocks in it. You know, all you had to do was ask and I would have introduced you. You are just lucky that we still won with my best point guard distracted by the beating you inflicted upon him!" Barry had heard the entire story from Grant and knew the boy was equally taken with Sydney as she was with him. Sydney had always been hard to read because she kept a mask in place all the time. In fact, the only one who knew her the best was Maria and he usually took his clues from her.

"Barry, it was an accident and I wasn't trying to meet him. He called me an angel? Barry quit teasing me. He never said that." Sydney was secretly hoping that Grant had said that and that he meant it when he said that he wanted to see her again real soon.

"Syd, the angel remark was straight from Grant's mouth and he also wanted me to give you a message. He would like you to wait for him to come out of the locker room. He wants to talk to you before you leave. Now if you ask me, you either inflicted a concussion on that boy so that he isn't thinking straight or you have driven him to distraction." Barry took his wife's hand and grabbed her van keys from the side pocket of her purse. Throwing them to Sydney, he said, "Here, you are going to need these. I will gladly take my lovely wife home. I may even treat her to coffee and dessert to celebrate our narrow victory. How does the

Dessert Factory sound? The babysitter isn't expecting us right away, is she?"

"No, she's actually staying the night and Pastor Steve will pick her up in the morning to take her to the youth retreat. It was easier for Cindy to stay because it will be closer for the bus. With an added bonus of we don't have to worry about what time we have to get home. Now let's roll and leave Sydney to fret about what she is going to say as she awaits her new beau." With that, Maria turned and directed Barry towards the door. "Stay out as late as you want we won't be waiting up for you and if you get home before us, don't wait up." Barry laughed and they left hand in hand looking forward to some time alone.

Sydney was left standing there and was struck with the last words that Maria had said. What would she say to Grant? She was starting to wonder if she should just flee and avoid the meeting when she looked up and saw him walking across the floor towards her. His hair was wet and he was dressed in a pair of faded jeans and a dark blue t-shirt that brought out the color of his eyes—those eyes held her in place and she was sure they were smiling at her.

"Hi."

"Hi."

"I'm glad you stayed"

"Yeah, me too. Sorry about your head Barry said you had quite a large bump." Sydney felt anticipation growing in her as she struggled to keep what was left of her composure intact.

Grant smiled and was relieved and thoroughly thrilled when he saw that she had stayed. She had been quite a distraction for him since the first glance at this blonde-haired beauty. She was like no other woman he had met and he loved her quick response and witty humor when she had hit him in the head. He was going to enjoy getting to know her. "Yep. I'm sporting quite the bump, thanks to you, but no hard feelings. I'm glad you hit me because now I get the opportunity to get to know you. How about some coffee? You do drink coffee, don't you?"

"Coffee? Yes, I drink coffee. Actually, you're talking to someone who lives on coffee and chocolate. I am a genuine coffee-holic, the stronger the better. No weak stuff for this gal. In fact, I carry my trusty coffee mug wherever I go…that's probably what you felt in my purse. I'd love to have coffee with you. Where do you want to go?"

"Well, a girl after my own heart! I too am a coffee-holic and I know this great little place called the Living Room Coffeehouse on First and Greenway."

"That's my favorite place! A great cup of coffee and a good book on one of their sofas and I'm set for at least an hour or two. I could meet you there. Maria left me her van so that she and Barry could have a night out to celebrate the victory."

"Well, then we have another thing in common because that is also my favorite place. How about I meet you there in ten minutes? I have to drop Chuck off because his sister left with the keys to his truck."

"Sure, ten minutes will be great; shall I order something for you?" Sydney's desire to flee had left and she now considered ten minutes apart as too long. This surprised her, for she had never felt this way about anyone before.

"Sure, that would be great. I'll have a Barcelona dark blend, no cream and no sugar. Oh yeah and make it an extra large, I want to stay awake for as long as it takes to get to know everything about Sydney Forrester. See you in ten." As Grant turned to leave, he too felt that ten minutes was going to be too long and also hoped that she felt the same way as he. He had never believed in love at first sight but now he wasn't so sure. This little blonde was stealing his heart and he only knew her name.

Sydney couldn't believe this! Barcelona dark blend was

her favorite too. He was more than she could ask for. Tall, dark, handsome and he liked the same coffee…this was definitely a match made in heaven. Well, Maria had been right—she, Sydney Ruth Forrester, was most definitely hooked on one Grant Gillman.

That night had changed her life. After they had talked for three hours over coffee she felt like she had known him her whole life. Two months later they were engaged and five months after that they were married in a small intimate wedding at Hope Christian Church. It was so hard to believe that it was seventeen years ago.

Sydney jolted back to reality and noticed the clock said nine forty-five. *Oh no, she only had forty minutes to get ready and get across town to her meeting. She would have to phone Maria from her cell phone and see if she had any lunch plans.* Sydney detoured through the kitchen so she could get a refill on her coffee to drink as she got ready. She surely hoped the meeting wouldn't run long because she wasn't sure if she had patience for all the bickering today.

CHAPTER THREE

The rain was steady but not heavy as Grant Gillman drove to work. It was late May and he hoped that his brothers were getting this moisture on the farm. Grant had talked to his brother Don the night before to see if they had been able to get all of the seeding done. Don seemed relieved to have finished the night before, so if they got this rain, it would start the crops off right. Although Grant had his own business, Gillman Homes and Renovations, he always liked to know what was happening at the farm. Sydney always teased him that he could take the boy off the farm but not the farm out of the boy. There was defiantly something special about living on a farm but Grant had never liked all the chores and endless hours on the tractor. Grant had gladly accepted the basketball scholarship and gone to college to explore other opportunities. It was there that he had met Sydney and life took on a whole new meaning.

Grant finished college with a degree in Engineering Design and Drafting Technology.

Grant then went to work for his bachelor uncle, Graham Gillman, who then owned Gillman Homes and Renovations. When Graham had retired ten years ago he sold the business to Grant for a reasonable price so that it would stay in the family. Grant enjoyed all the challenges of his own business and loved the fact that Sydney had been able to come work at the office as secretary, bookkeeper, and general helper. Grant was amazed that they worked so well together after hearing so many horror stories about couples that just couldn't master being co-workers. Grant was a blessed man and he thanked the Lord every day for the day he had met Sydney.

Sydney had captured his heart the moment that he had turned around to see who had hit him. Coffee after the game had only sealed the commitment to never let her out of his sight. Grant had shopped for the engagement ring after only one month of dating Sydney but had waited until their two-month anniversary to propose. Barry and Maria had helped Grant plan everything right down to the performance of Sydney's favorite song. Grant would never forget that night.

It was the championship game between Spring Hills Bulls and the Brooksville Buffaloes—the very team they had been playing when Grant had first met Sydney. Maria was to make sure that Sydney didn't leave during half time for her usual coffee and chocolate bar. As far as Grant was concerned, Maria had the most difficult job because nothing could get between Sydney and her coffee. Barry had the next most challenging job. Barry had to get an entire team of basketball players to sing Unchained Melody. For these guys, finding any key near the right key was going to be a challenge. Grant felt sympathy for Barry because these guys were definitely basketball players and not singers.

Finally the night of the big game came and Grant was a little nervous. Grant had seen Sydney come in with Maria. Sydney had waved and given him one of those smiles that caused his pulse to quicken and is heart to race. Grant then noticed that she was wearing the same Bulls sweatshirt that she had worn two months ago. Sydney looked gorgeous with her blonde curls falling down around her shoulders. At that moment Grant was no longer nervous because he knew that life without her was unthinkable. Maria sat down next to Sydney and gave Grant a wink as Barry walked over to talk to the team. Now Grant had to try and keep his mind on the championship game at hand. Grant knew the first half was going to take forever. As half time approached Sydney got ready to go for coffee. She liked to slip out just before the buzzer to avoid the long lines.

As Sydney started to get up Maria put her hand on her arm. "Sit down, you don't need to go for coffee. I have a thermos of your favorite from that place you go to downtown. What's the name of it again?"

"The Living Room Coffeehouse?"

"Yep, that's the one. Bar-something blend and I also have two chocolate bars so all you have to do is get that coffee mug of yours out of your purse." Maria pulled a large thermos out of her purse and then produced two of Sydney's favorite milk chocolate and almond bars.

Surprised by all this, Sydney found her cup and handed it to Maria to fill. "Barcelona dark blend...how did you know that it was my favorite?"

"Oh, a little bird told me. Actually, I asked Grant so that you wouldn't have to fight the crowds." Maria was struggling with not grinning like an idiot because of what was going to happen next. She never thought that this would be so hard to keep from Sydney. Maria was bursting with happiness and excitement for Sydney and Sydney didn't even know.

Just then the buzzer sounded signaling the end of the first half and the announcers voice came across the loud speakers.

"Attention Ladies and Gentlemen, if you could just remain in your seats for a few minutes, the Bulls have a presentation they would like to make. Thank you for your cooperation."

Barry and the team made their way to the center of the court and turned to face the stands where Maria and Sydney were seated.

"Maria, is this the presentation of the funds they raised for the pediatrics unit at the hospital?" Sydney had helped when the call went out for baking for the Bulls Annual Garage and Bake Sale for Charity. The team had set a record for funds raised and had chosen the pediatrics unit to receive the funds.

"No, I think they will make that presentation next week at the banquet." Maria was ready to explode and if the team didn't hurry she was going to ask Sydney for Grant.

Just then Barry walked to the front of the team and faced them. Acting like a choir conductor, Barry had half the team kneel and produce a single red rose from behind their backs. The music for Unchained Melody began and the team started to sing as Barry led them.

"Oh my love, my darling, I hunger for your touch a long lonely time. Time goes by so slowly and time can do so much. Are you still mine?"

Sydney would never forget the sound of fifteen basketball players trying to hit the right notes to one of her favorite oldie songs. Although she was a little confused why they were doing this at all.

"Maria, did the team lose a bet or something?"

"No, not that I know of. I guess we just have to wait until the boys finish butchering a classic to find out what is going on." Maria couldn't believe how badly the team was really doing although she had to give them and A+ for effort. Some of the guys were really getting into the song.

"I need your love, I need your love, Godspeed your love to me...."

As the song ended the game announcer handed a microphone to Barry.

"Sydney Forrester, could you please come to center

court." Barry was grinning from ear to ear as he tried to sound serious.

Sydney was speechless and even more confused as she turned to Maria and asked, "Maria, what's this about?"

"I'm not sure but you better go and find out."

Sydney rose and hesitantly walked to center court; she paused slightly as she stepped next to Barry. Sydney wasn't sure what was going on or why she had been singled out but she was sure that Barry was responsible in one way or another. Barry lived to try and embarrass her. Sydney just wasn't sure what he had up his sleeve.

"What's this about, Barry?"

Suddenly Sydney saw Grant emerge from behind the players carrying a dozen red roses. As Grant approached her, Sydney watched in disbelief as Grant dropped to one knee right in front of her. Barry held the microphone close to Grant.

"Sydney Forrester, I love you and every moment without you is like an eternity. Will you marry me?" Grant immediately saw the answer in her eyes and thought that there was no way she could look more beautiful. The entire gymnasium became so quiet that you could hear a pin drop as they all waited for the answer.

"Yes, oh yes, Grant I will marry you!" Sydney was in Grants arms before he could place the ring on her finger. The entire gymnasium erupted in cheers as the team gathered around the couple.

Sydney leaned closer to Grant's ear so that he could hear her and said "I'll get you back for embarrassing me this way, someday just you wait."

Grant held her close as he basked in the knowledge that she was his and whispered in her ear "It will be my pleasure to wait forever for your revenge as long as we are together. I love you, Syd."

Grant smiled as he remembered the fateful supper not

quite a year and a half later when Sydney's revenge finally came. Sydney was eight months pregnant with Brendan and they had been invited to the Bennett's for supper. Sydney had warned Grant that Jesse, Barry and Maria's oldest daughter, would be cooking the supper. Grant was warned that under no circumstance was he to say anything negative about the meal. Little did Grant know but the entire Bennett family was present and also eager participants.

Everyone was seated around the table as Jesse carried covered platters and bowls to the table. Grant remembered wondering why everything was covered and hoped the meal was more of a surprise for everyone than a hidden disaster waiting to be revealed. Jesse appeared nervous but excited about her first meal. Barry asked the blessing which seemed a little longer than normal.

When the blessing was over, Jesse looked directly at Grant and asked, "Grant would you be the first to taste everything for me?"

Not wanting to hurt her feelings and feeling a little hesitant, Grant reluctantly replied in the affirmative. Sydney squeezed his leg to let him know that he had made the right decision. Jesse came around the table to stand beside Grant. Just then Jesse lifted the lid off the first bowl and Grant's nose was assaulted by a smell that caused his stomach to protest. Jesse smiled as she dished up a thick, lumpy, green concoction that was even less appetizing in appearance than the odor had been.

"Grant, remember, I want the truth about how this tastes. My dad would just tell me it tastes great because he is my dad. That's why I picked you to go first." Jesse was performing her part flawlessly. Sydney was proud.

Grant looked to Barry for support but only received a grimace as he mouthed the words, "Good luck, buddy." Grant carefully took a forkful and brought it slowly to his mouth. His nose and stomach were protesting the nearness of the green goop. As Grant placed it in his mouth, he had all he could do to keep from spewing it across the room. The taste was even more repulsive then the odor.

Sydney again squeezed his leg and asked, "Well, Grant, how is Jesse's potato casserole? I know she worked all afternoon on it. She created this masterpiece all on her own."

"These are potatoes?" Grant asked as he struggled to swallow the disgusting mixture Sydney looked at him giving him, the "don't hurt her feelings" look, and Jesse looked like she was going to burst into tears.

"Jesse, this is one of the best potato casseroles that I have tasted, really." At that moment Grant would have done anything to keep from hurting Jesse but he wondered if his stomach could endure whatever awaited him in the other covered bowls.

Grant struggled to take another bite of the green potatoes casserole when the whole table broke out into laughter. Barry was laughing so hard his eyes were watering. Maria was bent over in gales of laughter while Sydney struggled to say something as she laughed. "I got you, Grant; now my revenge is complete." Sydney continued to laugh along with the entire family as Maria lifted the lids revealing one of Grant's favorite meals.

At that moment it dawned on Grant that he had been the brunt of a well-orchestrated plot to get him back for embarrassing Sydney. Grant had to admire her patience and ingenuity.

"So, I guess the wait is over. To be honest, I had completely forgotten and had thought you had too. I guess I was wrong." Grant smiled and handed his plate to Jesse. "Well, now I know this is not for human consumption, please help yourself."

"Are you kidding? I know what's in there." Jesse took his plate and brought a new one so that he could enjoy the real meal and the rest of the evening.

Those were the days—now it seemed that they were too busy for so many things. Grant was concerned for Sydney, the dreams were becoming more frequent, and he just didn't know what to do. Grant hoped that Sydney had been able to rest some this morning and hoped that his picking up the children and supper would alleviate some of the stress she must be under.

Grant thought about the previous night and wondered what was worrying her so much that she would have such frightful dreams. Grant thought about Maria and their friendship. He would have to remember to phone Maria and tell her about last night. Maybe she could help Sydney, especially when she seemed to not trust him for help and was reluctant to ask God for help.

Grant was approaching the intersection of Greenway and Broad when he decided to turn and stop by the church to talk to Pastor Steve. Work could wait; he had to pray for his wife. Grant felt an overwhelming need to bring his wife before the throne of grace and he could think of nowhere better than church. If Grant remembered correctly, Pastor Steve was usually in his office on Tuesday mornings and spent the afternoons doing visitation. Grant mentally reviewed his schedule and rearranged it so that he could spend some extra time talking to Pastor Steve. Grant reached for his cell phone as he pulled into the church parking lot and parked.

He dialed the first of his appointments, knowing they wouldn't mind coming in after lunch. Just as Grant was finishing the last phone call Pastor Steve stepped out the door and waved for him to come in. Grant jumped out of the truck and headed to the church.

"So what brings you by this morning, Grant? This is a little out of your way." Pastor Steve smiled but his eyes betrayed his concern for Grant.

"Well, I need to pray and I thought that you wouldn't

mind praying with me." Grant reached out and shook Pastor Steve's hand.

" No, that is one thing I never mind doing. Come Grant, let's take your concerns before God. There is no one more qualified to take care of them."

CHAPTER FOUR

Sydney pulled into the church parking lot for her ten-thirty meeting with just seconds to spare. The rain had slowed her down greatly for the simple fact that she hated to drive when it rained. Sydney was sure God had it in for her. Of all the days for it to rain, it had to be the day when she needed to sit in the sun and gather her thoughts. Some days she felt like she was going crazy. Sydney was a master at keeping her emotions hidden from those she loved but last night she just about let everything spill to Grant. Although she had been dealing with the dreams for years, they were becoming more frequent and more real with each one. Sydney was sure that something was going to happen soon or else the dreams wouldn't bother her so much.

"You're worrying too much, Sydney, now calm yourself and let's get some control here so you can go to this meeting." Sydney grabbed her oversized purse and shoved her daybook and cell phone inside. *"Okay here we go, composed and ready to face the world once again."* Sydney jumped out of her Ford Expedition and headed towards the door of the church. The rain was just enough that by the time she reached the door her semi-controlled curls were

nothing but a mass of frizz, causing her to wonder if anything else could go wrong today.

As Sydney walked into the church kitchen she realized that she was the last one to show up. Grabbing a mug from the tray she filled it up and thought again that she was going to have to buy the church some decent coffee. Heading to a chair at the far end of the table she set down her coffee and dug through her purse for an elastic band to get her hair out of her face.

"So ladies, what have you decided without me?" Sydney sat down beside Angela Sampson and hoped the meeting would be short and there would be no major disagreements over anything.

"Oh nothing, we really haven't talked about anything, yet anyway. You arrived just in time." Nancy Whitmore smiled as she proceeded to call the meeting to order. Nancy was the women's ministry president and had been for the last five years. Nancy's husband was the church board president, Saul, and compared to Nancy, he was quiet and easy to get along with. According to Sydney, things were run Nancy's way or no way and this caused Sydney's rebellious nature to be on the alert. Something about that lady just rubbed Sydney the wrong way and she really had to work at not being petty about things around Nancy.

"Well, the first thing that we need to discuss is how much money we can budget for a speaker and whom that speaker will be. I have already talked to Samantha Ross and she is free that weekend and she charges five hundred dollars plus traveling expenses. I personally think this is very inexpensive and she is my favorite speaker." Nancy continued to rattle on about Samantha Ross and expound on her qualities, trying to gain support for her choice.

"Well, who do you think she wants to speak at the retreat?" Sydney whispered to Angela, "What was the point of contacting Speakers Inc. to inquire about speakers if she already had on picked out?" Sydney was growing more irritated by the moment.

"You and I both know that Nancy will have her way with this weekend and it will be all about Nancy." Angela smiled and was glad they were at the far end of the table so that Nancy couldn't hear them. "Touché!" Sydney always enjoyed Angela's sense of humor.

Angela and her husband Rob had moved to Spring Hills about a year ago from Chicago. Rob was an electrician and was working for a large company, making a great living for himself and his new wife. But their lives changed after Angela had been attacked on her way home from work. Angela still walked with a limp after her attacker had tried to run her over with her own car, breaking her leg and shattering her knee. Angela had endured several surgeries and months of physical therapy. Rob had insisted that they move to a smaller town. Soon after they had moved, Grant had hired Rob to do some electrical work and a bond had been formed. The two couples had gotten to know each other quite well and had spent a lot of time together over the past year. Sydney was amazed that Angela had no bitterness and actually had sent a Gideon Bible to her attacker while he was in jail. Sydney just couldn't understand why this had happened to Angela. Sydney knew that she wouldn't have been that forgiving of her attacker or of God.

"Well, I think that she has rattled on long enough. Now it's my turn." Sydney gave Angela a devilish smile as she turned to face Nancy.

"Actually Nancy, when I contacted Speakers Inc. as we agreed that I would do at the last meeting, they told me that they have a speaker here in town that is also available that weekend. Her name is Courtney Morrison and she has written numerous Bible study books. Frances, the lady I talked to at Speakers Inc. said that Courtney would only ask for an honorarium, as well as traveling expenses." Sydney leaned over and produced a couple of books from her bag and laid them on the table.

"I took the liberty of picking up a couple of her Bible studies from Karen at the Bible bookstore. Karen highly recommended the studies and said that we could return them after the meeting. As you can see most of her studies deal with God's love and grace which is our theme for the retreat." With that, Sydeny sat back and smiled and waited for the outcome.

"Well, I don't know about the rest of you but an honorarium would fit our budget better than five hundred dollars. The fact that this Courtney has written on God's love and that it is our theme makes me think she might be the speaker that would be best." Dorothy Hamilton was usually the voice of reason in the group and Sydney was relieved when she had volunteered to sit on the retreat committee. Dorothy had lived alone since her husband Frank had died of cancer five years ago. Dorothy's daughter, Katherine, was a doctor at the Spring Hills General Hospital and came to church with her mom when she wasn't on call. Sydney had always appreciated Dorothy's insight and was looking forward to getting to know Katherine better. Sydney had only met her a couple of times but was always impressed with how much Katherine was like her mother.

"Well, I think that we need to think about this some more. Maybe I should talk to this Courtney before we decide. Samantha was more than willing to come and I think that she would do very nicely. Let's take some time to think about this and we can vote on it at the next meeting." Nancy seemed more than a little annoyed that things were not going as smoothly as she had planned. "Let's move on to our budget. Theresa, do you have the numbers from last year so that we have some guideline for this year's budget?"

"Just a moment, Nancy. I think that waiting for our next meeting might be too late for us to chose a speaker. Besides, we need to know what we are going to spend on a speaker before we can set the budget for other items." Dorothy turned to Theresa and asked "Wasn't the speaker the largest part of the budget last year?"

"Actually it was; we had to fly her in from Denver plus pay her speaker fee. We had to raise the cost of the weekend just to cover her expenses. The women didn't seem to mind the extra cost because the speaker was really great." Theresa was a quiet, soft-spoken woman in her forties. Theresa had never been married and taught half-time at the local high school. The kids loved this mild-mannered, petite brunette who taught physics and math. Brendan was in Theresa's math class last semester and said that it was the first time he really understood math. Sydney knew that Theresa loved to teach and had a way of connecting with the kids and teaching in a way that they could understand even the most complex problems.

"Well, I guess we could have a vote on the two ladies presented today, although I don't think we know enough about this Courtney to have a fair vote." Nancy was not pleased that Dorothy had foiled her plans. Nancy had hoped to delay the vote and book Samantha anyway. When the next meeting came she would just say that she had to make an executive decision in order to not lose a speaker. In the end she was sure that no one would care and would be happy with Samantha. Regardless, Nancy remained confident that she had shared enough about Samantha to gain a majority of the vote.

"I know that I am ready to vote after what you have shared about Samantha and seeing Courtney's books. What about the rest of you ladies?" Dorothy looked around the table and realized that all the ladies were nodding in agreement. "Nancy, if you would call a vote, I think the ladies have agreed to vote today."

"Very well. All in favor of Samantha Ross for speaker at

our Fall Retreat, raise your hand." Nancy raised her hand and noted that only two other ladies raised theirs as well. Nancy did not like the way that this vote was going. "All those in favor of Courtney Morrison, raise your hand." Every other hand in the room was raised and Nancy realized that she was not getting the speaker she wanted for her perfect weekend.

"Well, I guess that Courtney Morrison will be our speaker for retreat. Sydney, would you be so kind as to book her for the weekend?"

"Yes, I will do that today." Sydney had to keep from grinning as she turned and winked at Angela.

"Look at the time! I think that we should wait for our next meeting to discuss decorations and the budget. I have to get to a lunch meeting." Nancy didn't wait for any agreement and started to pack her things. "Our next meeting will be two weeks from today on the eighteenth, ten thirty here at the church. Well, I must be off, I'll see you ladies on Sunday at church." With that Nancy was out the door and the meeting came to an end.

"Now that was odd. I've never seen her leave a meeting so fast." Angela placed both hands on the table as she struggled to lift her eight-month pregnant body out of the chair. "I guess Nancy doesn't take defeat very well. Sydney, please tell me this pregnancy won't last forever and that there will be an end?"

"Yes, there will be an end, although for the next month you will feel like you are going to be big forever. And no, Nancy does not take defeat well. I think this is the first time I have seen that she didn't get her own way." Sydney stood and helped Angela. "Just think, in a month you'll be able to let Rob carry the baby all the time. I think you have carried this little one enough for a while. How is your leg? I know you said last week that it was cramping up on you."

"About as well as can be expected. The extra weight has

caused it to ache more but I try not to let Rob know. He makes me sit and do nothing and that just drives me crazy. I have too much to do to get ready for this little one." Angela never complained and that amazed Sydney. If anyone had a right to complain it was Angela and yet she was one of the happiest and most content women Sydney had ever met.

Just then Sydney's cell phone rang. Grabbing the phone out of her purse she excused herself from Angela and answered it.

"Hello."

"Hi there, how is the most beautiful woman in the world?"

"Now you're just being silly. What are you up to and where are you?" Sydney loved when Grant called—just his voice could calm her and cheer her day.

"Well, I'm just leaving the office and was wondering if you had plans for lunch. I was thinking that lunch with my lovely wife would be the best appointment I've had all day." Grant suddenly realized that she was probably at her retreat meeting. "Are you still at your meeting?"

Sydney waved goodbye to Angela and Dorothy then turned to pack her purse as she continued to talk to Grant. "My meeting just finished and no, I don't have plans for lunch. I was going to phone Maria but my morning has been a little rushed and I forgot. I thought I would stop by there after lunch and see if she was home. So I'm yours for lunch. Any place special you have in mind?"

Sydney had just reached the doors to the church when she noticed a truck sitting out side the front door. Upon closer inspection, there sat Grant smiling at her talking on his cell phone.

"I was thinking someplace with really great deserts. Have any ideas? I know that you and Maria have tested every place in town that serves any form of chocolate." Grant loved to surprise her. Grant had been driving by when he noticed Syd's SUV sitting in the parking lot. Thinking lunch with Syd would be far better than lunch alone, he reached for his phone to call her. When she had said that she was done, Grant had pulled up in front of the doors so he could see her face.

"I thought you said that you had just left the office?" Sydney was always surprised at how thoughtful Grant could be. He always seemed to know what to do to cheer her. "There is this little café on Broadway that makes all their own desserts. They have a great apple pie."

"My favorite! Lets go there. You can ride with me and I'll bring you back to your vehicle later. How do you know they have great pie—you only eat chocolate?"

"Maria said that Barry has tried the apple pie and that it was very good." Sydney jumped into Grant's truck feeling that things were starting to look up. Maybe the worst was behind her and she was just worrying for nothing.

"Well, Barry sure knows his apple pie. Sit back and relax, my dear, and let me take you away for a quiet lunch rendezvous." Grant pulled out of the parking lot, looking forward to a little alone time with his wife. Sydney sat back and closed her eyes, thinking about how lucky she was to have such a great husband.

CHAPTER FIVE

"Madam Gillman, what a lovely surprise! It has been nearly two weeks since you and Madam Bennett have graced us with your presence. What a great day for you to visit! I have created a new dessert that has wondrous layers of caramel and milk chocolate, whipped cream and some chunks of baked cheesecake all in a magnifique chocolate mousse. I have not named this dessert yet but I would love for you to taste it and give me a true chocoholic's opinion." Hans Von Randal, a large balding man with a heavy French accent, was the owner of Café Magnifique. Hans and Marie had moved from Geneva, Switzerland three years ago and opened this small café where they could create desserts and visit with customers. Hans had worked at a large hotel in Geneva as head chef, while Marie had stayed at home and raised their nine children. Most of their children had married and moved to different parts of Europe except for Patrice, their youngest. Patrice had moved to America to go to college, and after meeting Pierre Bonet, she had moved to Spring Hills. Patrice was a legal secretary for her now fiancé Pierre. Hans and Marie had given in to Patrice's pleas to come and visit.

Once there, they had fallen in love with the area and moved as soon as all the loose ends were tied up in Geneva. The Café had become an instant success because of Hans and Marie's friendly atmosphere. People who entered the café left feeling like they had been visiting in a good friends home instead of eating at a restaurant.

"Hans, by now you should know that I would never turn down anything with chocolate. The fact that you have added all the rest makes it even more tempting. It sounds like chocolate heaven, Maria will be disappointed that I was able to taste it before her." Sydney and Maria had enjoyed coffee here every week since it had opened but oddly, Grant had never been here. "You will get to meet my husband Grant today as he has whisked me away from my meeting for a quiet rendezvous."

"Oh, Sydney, how romantic. All I can get Hans to do is bake me more desserts. Do I look like I need more dessert?"

Marie had just come out of the kitchen carrying a fresh pot of coffee. Marie was an attractive woman with her beautiful gray hair. Marie was slightly overweight but blamed it on her husband's wondrous cooking skills.

"I heard you come in and knew you would need some coffee. Now does your husband drink coffee or would he like something else, my dear?"

"Her husband drinks only good coffee. Just like his wife taught him." Grant had just walked through the door from parking his truck. "And from the sounds of the conversation, my wife must come here a lot if you know about her coffee habits."

"Bon jour, Monsieur Gillman, it is a privilege to finally meet you. My name is Hans and this is my wife Marie. Your wife graces us with her presence weekly with Madame Bennett, so yes, we know that she loves chocolate and coffee." Hans smiled as he brought menus for Sydney and Grant. "Now do you love chocolate as much as your beautiful wife or is there something else that would interest you?"

"Well, I do not have quite the sweet tooth that my wife has but I have heard that you make apple pie." Grant already loved the quaint little café and knew that he was going to enjoy visiting with the owners.

"Oh. Monsieur Gillman, you are a man after my own heart. Apple pie is my favorite and no one makes better apple pie than my lovely Marie. I will make sure that there is a piece ready for you after your lunch." Hans was poring water for his guests when he leaned over to Grant and said, "I may even have a piece with you so that we can get to know each other. It has taken Madame Gillman far too long to bring you in. We men have to stick together, you know." Hans laughed.

"Oh, Hans you must not be so nosy, the Gillman's are here for a quiet lunch. Did you not hear Sydney when she first came in? Now let us go and let these dear people decide what they would like for lunch." Marie grabbed Hans by the arm and led him back to the kitchen.

"So you come here once a week with Madame Bennett." Grant had to laugh when he said Madame because it just didn't seem to fit the Maria he knew.

"I knew that you would like this place but we just never go out by ourselves much anymore. This was such a nice surprise and thank you for the extra rest this morning, although I took full advantage and was just about late for my meeting." Sydney browsed the menu even though she already knew what she was going to have.

"So, how did your meeting go? Nancy sure took off in a hurry; she came out of the church like a woman on a mission. Did everything go okay or did you ruffle her feathers again?" Grant knew how much Nancy rubbed Sydney the wrong way and was amazed that there weren't more confrontations.

"Well, she wasn't real happy that the vote for the speaker

was called today and that her speaker wasn't chosen. But other than that, she was her usual self. She bolted right after the vote so we'll see how she is at church on Sunday." Sydney hoped that she would just get over it and carry on with the plans, but she had a feeling that they hadn't heard the last on the speaker matter.

"Well my dear, have you decided what you would like for lunch or should I give you lovebirds another few minutes?" Marie had come out of the kitchen with the coffee pot to refill their cups.

"I'll have the roast beef dip with fries. I will also have a piece of the best apple pie in the world afterward, please."

"My husband has been talking to you. So no chocolate for you, just some plain apple pie?" Marie was always flattered when her husband raved about her pie but she never liked to let on.

"Oh no, apple pie is never plain to me! There is nothing better than a great piece of apple pie, especially with a little ice cream."

"You and my husband are two of a kind when it comes to dessert. He can create the most fabulous desserts but he only wants my apple pie when its time for him to eat. Never will I understand men. Monsieur Bennett is the same way. Now Sydney my dear, what would you like?"

"Marie, I will just have the Greek salad with.."

"No onions, I remember my dear. Would you like me to get you a piece of that chocolate creation in the kitchen for dessert?"

"Of course I will have a piece. You know I couldn't turn down anything that sounds that good. Thank you, Marie." Sydney watched Marie head back to the kitchen and remembered why she loved this place so much. Hans and Marie reminded her so much of her grandparents.

"They remind you of your grandparents, don't they?" Grant knew from the look on her face who she was thinking about and was glad that she had found this place and this wonderful older couple. Grant had remembered how hard it had been on Sydney when both her grandparents were killed in an automobile accident. Hans and Esther Forrester had been on their way to Phoenix for vacation when a drunk driver had crossed the centerline and hit them head-on. Both of them had been killed instantly while the driver of the other car had walked away with just a broken arm. Sydney had been the one the police had phoned when they couldn't reach her parents. Grant still remembered watching her as she sank to the floor, gasping for breath while she dropped the phone beside her. The next few years had brought on a lot of nightmares. They had subsided and were now back full force from what he could tell. *Please God, help me to know how to help her through whatever is haunting her. Give me wisdom and your guidance in this.*

"Yes, they do remind me of them. I still think of them a lot and miss them terribly." Sydney's heart ached still at the memory of the accident that had claimed the lives of her grandparents. She would never forget the phone call or of having to tell her parents of what had happened.

"How are you feeling today, Syd? Your dream last night really shook you up and frankly, it shook me up a little." Grant had thought about nothing else all morning. Stopping at the church to pray had helped, but now seeing how vulnerable she was, it was all he could do to leave it in the Lord's hands.

"Grant you know that it wasn't anything serious. I'm fine now. Let's not talk about it and just enjoy this wonderful lunch together. So how was your morning? Have you seen Rob today? Angela is really suffering with her leg. I really feel for her; I wish there was something more I could do for her." Sydney didn't like lying to Grant but she didn't want him to worry. Worst of all, she didn't want him to think that she was going crazy. Sydney just wanted Grant to be happy and not to worry about her because he had enough to worry about with the business.

"Well, my morning was slack. I rebooked all my appointments to this afternoon or tomorrow and spent some time at the church." Grant didn't want to let Sydney off the hook that easy. He wanted to know what was bothering his wife and help her get through whatever it was. He hated it when she changed the subject and tried to make light of her nightmares.

"Was Pastor Steve getting a quote on renovations to the church? I heard that the building committee wanted some quotes. That would be great if you got the job, wouldn't it?" Sydney was feeling pleased that she had been able to get Grant from pressing her about her dreams. She felt a little guilty but knew that it was for the best.

"No, it wasn't about the renovations. I went to the church to pray. I was worried about you and felt like I needed to pray for you."

"You didn't tell Pastor Steve about my dreams, did you?' Sydney was horrified that someone might know about her dreams. It was bad enough that she suspected that Grant did not believe that they were falling dreams anymore. Panic started to rise and her chest began to get tight at the thought that people might think that she was crazy. Grant wouldn't need an excuse then to have her committed.

"Sydney, I didn't tell Pastor Steve anything. I just said that I had some concerns I wanted to bring before the Lord. He shared some verses with me about approaching the throne of Grace confidently and about leaving my concerns in God's hands. Then we prayed. Your name was only brought up in respect to the meeting this morning. What has you so upset?" Grant saw the panic in her eyes and wondered what was so upsetting that she was scared to share it with the pastor and himself.

"Grant, I just don't think that some silly little dreams are something that everyone needs to know about you know?

You don't need to worry about me, I'm fine. Really, I am. Please, let's just not talk about this anymore? I'm okay." Sydney was relieved to see Hans and Marie coming out of the kitchen with their lunch.

"Here's your lunch. I hope that you enjoy it and I will get you both some more coffee." Marie set the Greek salad down in front of Sydney and turned to go get the pot of coffee.

"Here you go, Monsieur, I hope it is to your liking. I will go see that your apple pie is ready for ice cream as soon as you are finished." Hans lingered at the table smiling.

"Hans, don't just stand there gawking at them! Let them eat in peace and you go get those dishes done in the kitchen." Marie knew that Hans would just sit down and visit if she let him. Marie filled the cups and then grabbed Hans and pulled him back to the kitchen. "Come Hans, lets go to the kitchen"

"You are no fun, woman, " Hans complained as Marie escorted him to the back.

"I'll show you fun old man now get those dishes done." Marie laughed as Hans slapped her on the behind as he headed to the dishwasher.

"I see why you enjoy this place so much. Is there always this much entertainment?"

"Hans loves to annoy Marie and it does prove to be very entertaining. Your sandwich looks really good. I haven't tried one of those yet." Sydney speared a piece of tomato from her salad as she eyed all the roast beef on his sandwich.

"Stop eyeing my lunch, you have your own. Is it my fault that you chose a salad over some great roast beef?" Grant had to laugh because Sydney usually thought that his meal looked better than hers when they'd come. It never failed that before long, she would ask for a bite and he would in turn end up eating half of her salad.

"So you're going to let me have a bite so I know whether I should have one of those next time?" Sydney smiled sweetly knowing that Grant would eventually relent and let her have a taste.

"I can vouch for the taste and you must have one of these next time. Stop looking at me with those puppy-dog eyes. You know that I can't say no when you do that. Oh for Pete's sake, have a taste! By the way, I wish that you would order salads that I like if I'm going to end up eating half of it." Grant smiled and handed Sydney half of his sandwich. She had won this time but he wasn't finished talking about her dreams. He would just have to get her alone tonight after the children were in bed to talk. "How is it that you eat a lunch item and a dessert when you come with Maria? You can never eat both when you are with me?'

Sydney smiled and started to giggle, "Well, for starters, Maria and I always split a meal so that we can have our own dessert."

"Now you tell me. Why couldn't we have done that? Next time, my dear, we will split the sandwich and then you can have your dessert." Grant sat back and laughed with his wife, deciding to just enjoy the rest of the meal and this short time with the woman he loved so much.

CHAPTER SIX

S ydney smiled to herself as she drove up the driveway to Maria's house. Her lunch with Grant had started out a little scary when he had pushed for answers about why she was so scared last night but after lunch was served, he seemed to forget about it and they had enjoyed a lovely meal together. Hans and Marie had even joined them for dessert when the lunch crowd had dispersed and they had a few minutes. Grant and Hans had seemed to hit it off. They had common ground when it can to teasing their wives. Grant had loved the apple pie and had complimented Marie too many times to count. Hans had beamed at the compliments, adding his own every now and again. As for the chocolate dessert Sydney had eaten, well, she was so full that she thought she was going to burst and she would have died a chocoholic's dream. Hans had insisted that she bring a piece for Madame Bennett so that she could give her professional opinion. Sydney still wasn't accustomed to being called Madame but found it only endeared her to the Von Randal's more.

Sydney turned off her SUV and reached for her purse, throwing the cell phone in and reached for the dessert for

Maria. Sydney smiled and felt a rush of joy when she remembered how Grant had kissed her goodbye telling her how much he loved her and to have a great visit with Maria. Grant could still make her melt when he kissed her. He had dropped her off and reminded her he would pick up the kids and pizza. Throwing her another kiss, he had driven off to his appointment with some prospective renovation clients.

"Maria, have I got a treat for you! Put some good coffee on and grab a fork; you are going to absolutely love this!" Sydney knocked once and entered the house. Kicking off her shoes, she headed for the kitchen. Maria and Barry's house had at one time been too small for them and their four children but now that only Glenda was at home, they had plenty of room. Maria had always had a flair for decorating and loved to work on new projects.

"Syd, I'll be right out, I'm just cleaning my hands. I painted my bathroom; you have to come and see what it looks like. It is a little bolder than I had expected but I think I'm going to like it. Did you say that you brought me something?"

"Yep! I brought you a new dessert from Hans and Marie. They say hello to you and wonder how come you weren't with me today. I'll put on some coffee and then come and see your bathroom. By the way, which bathroom?" Sydney put the dessert on the table and headed to the coffee maker. Everything was still in the same place as when she had lived there more that seventeen years earlier.

"I painted the bathroom in Barry's and my bedroom. The one with the dark blue tile and counter top. I also painted the cupboards in here and bought material for the window." Maria was still scrubbing the paint off her hands. It didn't matter how careful she was, it seemed that she always had paint from her head down to her toes when she painted. Maria said a quick prayer for guidance as she visited with Sydney today. Grant had phoned her earlier and told her that Sydney had had yet another nightmare. Maria was worried about Sydney and Grant. Although Sydney had never told her about the dreams, she had seen the fear in Sydney's eyes whenever she had come to visit the day after. Grant had kept Maria posted on all the dreams and was very worried about her. Maria knew that Grant wanted to help Sydney but she was resistant to tell anyone what was going on. Maria hoped that maybe today Sydney would open up, but Maria knew she couldn't push or that would just close the door even tighter.

"Maria, I love it." Sydney had to admire the color choice. The once brown cupboards were now white and the walls a very pale shade of yellow. With the navy blue tiles the contrast was striking. "Is this the material that you picked out for the window?" Sydney fingered the navy blue cotton with tiny yellow roses sprinkled through out.

"Yes, don't you just love the contrast of the yellow roses in the navy background? I was a little hesitant with yellow walls and the navy tiles but I really like the way that it has turned out. So you said that Hans sent me something?" Maria wiped her hands and headed down the hall to the kitchen. "Has Hans been creating again?"

"You're going to love this new creation. He hasn't named it yet but I personally think 'Death by Chocolate' would suit it perfectly." Sydney followed Maria to the kitchen noticing that the aroma of the coffee was drifting down the hall.

"So since you didn't take me to lunch I'm assuming you were able to get Grant to go with you?" Maria poured two cups of coffee and set them on the table. After retrieving the cream from the fridge and two forks from the drawer, Maria sat at the table with Sydney.

"Oh. Maria, it was such a surprise when Grant phoned to go for lunch. Then as I was talking to him and heading for my car there He was right in front of the church doors. Hans and Grant got along way too well. I can see that if Barry was included we women would be in for real trouble."

"I know what you mean. Barry and Hans or Barry and Grant is enough trouble already. The three of them would be too much to handle, I'm afraid. This is fabulous. Hans has certainly outdone himself this time. I don't know how Marie can live with all this great food around all the time. I bet I'd weigh three hundred pounds if Barry cooked like this."

"I would be that or more. Your bathroom looks great I never would have thought of that. Where did you get the idea?" Sydney wasn't sure but she thought that Grant might have phoned Maria about the dream last night. Sydney was pretty sure that Maria knew every time that the dreams haunted her. Sydney's best course of action was to keep things light and try to keep the conversation away from herself.

"I was at the fabric store picking up some material for Glenda. Then I came across the navy cotton and just loved the yellow roses. You know how I love roses. Well when I saw the two colors together, my mind just started rolling. It saved me the hassle of having to paint all the tiles." Maria sipped her coffee and leaned back in her chair. Sydney did this every time that she had a dream—keep the conversation away from her. Maria only hoped that one day Sydney would trust one of them enough to let them know what was happening in her life. Maria knew that Sydney had taken the death of her grandparents really hard and although many of the details were sketchy, Maria knew that Sydney's other grandmother had been admitted to a psychiatric hospital. Sydney never talked about it and Maria wondered if things were starting to catch up with Sydney and she was going to have to deal with some of her past. Maria had always sensed that Sydney was running and wondered how long she could possibly keep on doing that.

Maria listened to Sydney recap the meeting at the church and about her lunch with Grant. *Lord, she is running*

*and I don't know how to help her. Give me the ears to hear
and the wisdom to know what is the real issue bothering
Sydney. I feel that things are starting to pile up on her and
that she is going to crash. Lord help her and may she see
how much you love her and have wondrous plans for her.*

"Maria, I can't believe how this afternoon has just flown
by. I really wanted to sit in your garden but the rain has put a
damper on that today. But it has been so nice just sitting here
and relaxing. It's already nearly five-thirty and Grant should
be home with the kids and pizza in just minutes. They're
going to beat me home. It's a good thing I wasn't making
supper today or it would be late." Sydney couldn't believe
she had spent the whole afternoon there. But then again
when Maria and she got together, time did have a way of
flying by. Sydney hadn't even thought about her dream for at
least two hours and that felt good—it seemed almost normal.

"I had better get some supper ready for Barry because
I'm sure he is not bringing home pizza. Glenda is going out
with David tonight so I won't have to worry about feeding
her. I think that scrambled eggs and toast will taste very
good tonight. Not that I am at all hungry after that great
dessert." Maria walked Sydney to the door, wishing there
was something that she could do or say to help her friend.

"You know, sometimes I think that eggs and toast is a
great supper, although my children are not real fond of that.
It doesn't look like the rain has let up at all today. I hope that
Grant is careful on the roads." Sydney slipped her shoes on
and grabbed her denim jacket.

"The rain makes everything smell so fresh and clean. I
love it when it rains. The rain seems to perk up all the plants
so much better than just sprinkling does." Maria reached
down and picked up Sydney's purse and handed it to her just
as the cell phone rang.

"That must be Grant. I bet he is home already and they
want to eat. I guess they will just have to start without me."

Sydney reached into her purse and pulled out her cell phone and answered it.

"Hello"

"Syd…. Syd …is that you?"

"Yes, it's me. Grant, is that you? What's wrong?"

"Syd…Syd…"

"Grant. Grant, are you there? What's happened?" Sydney's heart was pounding and panic was starting overwhelm her

"Syd…. I love you."

CHAPTER SEVEN

Grant had picked Brendan up from the school where he was having practice but because of the rain, it had turned into an afternoon of weight training. Needless to say, Brendan was not in a very happy mood by the time Grant had driven up to the school.

"Dad, I just don't understand why we have to do so much weight training? I mean, I'm in great shape. I run every day but still Coach keeps harping on me to keep pumping weights."

"Brendan, you know that Coach doesn't want you to get hurt and the best way to keep you from injury is to do some weight training." Grant knew that Brendan could put up with just about anything that was asked of him when it came to playing ball, but weights just drove Brendan crazy.

"Besides," Grant added, " this too shall pass, and before you know it, you'll be starting pitcher for the Cardinals and then you will appreciate all your hard work."

"Well right now, it seems like a waste of time and energy. So what kind of pizza are we getting?" Brendan was starving and if his mother were here she would tell him that he was always hungry. What could he say? He was a growing boy and needed to be fed more often.

"I think that we should wait until we have picked up your brother and sister before we decide. You know how upset Sarah Rose gets when she's left out of the decision making." Grant had to chuckle when Brendan rolled his eyes and let out his usual, disgusted sigh. Grant had seen that expression too many times since Brendan had become a teen. All Grant could do was chuckle because he remembered doing the same thing when he was that age. Even though Brendan would not admit it, Sarah Rose had him wrapped around her little finger. In fact, Sarah Rose had everyone in the family wrapped around her little finger.

Driving up to Patty Marshall's house, Grant noticed that Scott was just inside the door watching for them. Sarah Rose was probably telling Patty all about her day at school. Patty Marshall had offered to teach piano lessons for the Gillman's in order to make a little extra money. It had started out that she just wanted to put some money away for an anniversary trip for her husband Mike. Mike and Patty had been married for ten years and had only one child. Patty stayed home to raise Tyler so money had been tight. Patty and Mike had met the Gillman's when Grant had done some renovations in the Marshall's basement. This was where Grant had learned of Patty's desire to earn some extra cash. It worked out well for them because the Gillman's were looking for a piano teacher at the time. After the anniversary trip to Mexico, Patty realized that she enjoyed teaching the children. So she had kept on and now this was her second year teaching Sarah Rose and her seventh with Scott.

Brendan had only taken one year of lessons and then had declared to his parents that a baseball player did not need to know how to play piano and that guitar lessons would be more cool. Patty was sorry to see Brendan give up the piano because she said that he had the best posture and fingering of anyone she had taught.

Scott enjoyed the lessons and was starting to write some of his own music. Sydney complained that he played by ear more often then by reading the notes but Scott just told her that it was easier that way. Patty didn't seem too concerned when Sydney had talked to her about it. Patty said that God had given Scott the gift of a great ear for music and that she would just adjust her teaching to incorporate that special ability. Scott had thrived under Patty's instruction and played piano for all the young people's gatherings.

Sarah Rose loved all the attention from the music lessons and Patty adored Sarah Rose. Sarah Rose started playing and just loved it so much she started to practice songs farther along in the book than where Patty had taught her. Patty finally gave up and let Sarah Rose set the pace, which hadn't let up in two years. Sarah Rose could hardly get enough time to practice and was really put out when Scott demanded his own turn at the piano.

Scott ran out to the truck, followed closely by Sarah Rose and climbed in the back of Grant's extended cab truck. Brendan closed the door and they were off to Checker's Pizza Palace for supper.

"So Squirt, what kind of pizza do you want? Dad said that we had to wait to ask your opinion. Not that it really matters in the long run." Brendan moved his backpack to the center of the front seat and away from his feet.

"Well. My opinion does matter, no matter what you say, Brendan. I would like to have Hawaiian. Can I get my own pizza, Daddy? Please? Then I don't have to share." Sarah Rose sat in the middle of the back seat right next to Scott so that he could listen to her read her new book from the library. Sarah Rose loved to read and fifteen minutes of reading each night was just not enough for her. Scott was her favorite person to read to because he always seemed to have time for her. Brendan would sit with her but he never really listened to what she was reading.

"Sarah Rose, you always order Hawaiian and no one else likes it. You always get the pizza to yourself. What kind do you think your mother would like?" Grant shook his head every time they ordered pizza because Sarah Rose always wanted the same thing and always expressed concern that she was going to have to share. Grant had to admit that he liked to tease her that he now liked Hawaiian and that she would have to share with him. The boys both liked to tease her too, though she was certainly capable of antagonizing her brothers in return when she set her mind to it.

"Oh Daddy, Mommy would love the all meat one with black olives and tomatoes. I think you should get her one all for her own too." Sarah rose grabbed her new book from her Barbie backpack and opened it to the first page. "Scotty, are you ready to listen to my new book?"

"Yeah, I'll listen to your book. Move a little closer so I can see the pictures. Do you have your seatbelt on?" Scott pulled his seatbelt across and buckled it into place and then leaned over to help Sarah Rose.

"Brendan, could you run in and order the pizzas? Get a large all meat with half black olives and tomatoes, a small Hawaiian, and a large ham and pepperoni. Check to see if they still have the bread stick special and if they do, order two bread sticks with dipping sauce."

"Sure Dad, I'll be right back, two bread sticks right?" Brendan jumped out of the truck and was gone before Grant could answer. Grant sat back and watched Brendan walk into Checker's Pizza Palace. Grant knew that Brendan would not object to going in and ordering since his girl-friend, Amanda Cookson, worked there almost every evening that she wasn't busy at some sort of sports. Amanda and Brendan had noticed each other at camp the previous summer even though they'd been going to school together all their lives. Grant liked Amanda and was glad that Brendan was seeing a good Christian girl. When Grant and

Sydney had first found out, they had set out a few ground rules to which Brendan had protested at first. When he realized that Amanda's parents had set out even more ground rules for their daughter—many of which were the same as the Gillman's—Brendan had relented and abided by the rules with less complaining.

As Grant listened to Sarah Rose read to Scotty, he thought back to his afternoon and lunch with his wife. Sydney had been so surprised to see him sitting outside the door. Lunch at that café was one of the best he had had in a long time. Grant was going to have to remember the place when he had business lunches. Hans and Marie had to be the nicest couple and they really did remind him of Syd's grandparents. Grant had always loved to visit Sydney's grandparents. Hans and Esther Forrester had always made Grant feel welcome and part of their family. Grant couldn't remember a time when they had visited when Esther didn't have a pie in the oven or one that was cooling. Grant hoped that Sydney wouldn't have to go through that kind of trauma again for a very long time. Sydney rarely talked about her other grandmother, Ruth Stern, and from what he could gather, Syd had spent a lot of time at her place and had been very close to her. What had happened to her? Grant had never really been certain because the family didn't seem willing to talk about Grandma Ruth.

"Dad they had the bread stick special so I ordered two and here are the pizzas. This is going to be great. Do we have to wait till we get home to eat?" Brendan jumped into the truck and snapped his seatbelt in to place as he attempted to open one of the hot pizzas. "Wow, this Hawaiian looks great, I may have to try this one. Mmmmmmm."

"Don't you touch my pizza! Dad, Brendan is trying to eat my pizza." Sarah Rose attempted to hit Brendan with her book but the seat belt hindered her reach.

"Brendan, don't tease your sister and Sarah Rose, don't

hit. You know he doesn't like Hawaiian. Now sit back and read your book. Brendan, close the pizza because we're waiting until we get home." Grant pulled out into the street and headed home.

The rain had picked up since they left the pizza place and Grant had to speed up the wipers to keep up with the rain. As Grant headed up Twenty-sixth Avenue, he approached Second Street lights. The light was red and as they waited, Grant listened to Scott help Sarah Rose with a word she was having trouble with. The light changed to green and Grant proceeded across the intersection.

"DAD, WATCH OUT!!" Brendan yelled just as Grant saw the large gravel truck come barreling through the red light straight at them.

"Everyone, hold on!" Grant yelled. Grant knew they were going to be hit by the larger vehicle and thought that if he turned his own truck to go the same way as the gravel truck then maybe he could just glance off the truck instead of slamming into him head on. Grant swerved and it felt as if the next few moments slowed down like slow motion in a movie or on TV. Grant heard Sarah Rose screaming and Scotty yell, "Jesus, save us." The sound of crushing metal was deafening and Grant felt his whole body being thrown toward the dashboard. Then there was silence.

Grant opened his eyes and searing pain ripped through his head. Remembering what had happened, he turned to see how Brendan was.

"Brendan . . . Brendan, are you ok?"

"Dad, it hurts, it hurts really badly" his son weakly answered.

"Brendan, try not to move."

"Are you okay, Dad?"

"Yeah. My head hurts. Scotty . . . Sarah Rose . . . are you two okay?" Grant felt like things were growing more fuzzy and he struggled to keep his thought in focus.

"I don't know, Dad. Sarah Rose is leaning next to me crying and there seems to be a lot of blood back here."

Just then a man came around to where the driver's side window had been. "Are you okay? I called the ambulance so just sit tight and try not to move. "

"My name is Grant Gillman. Please, can you make sure that my children are alright?"

"Sure. My name is David O'Rielly and I'm a paramedic. I was following behind you and saw the whole thing. Mr. Gillman, are you having trouble focusing?" David leaned into the truck and looked at Grant's eyes.

"Yeah, a little. I think I may black out. Could you do something for me?"

"Sure Grant, what would you like?" David was getting concerned about Grant's condition and hoped the ambulance wasn't long in coming.

"Could you find my cell phone?" Grant felt like the world was starting to fade around him but he wanted to stay focused so that he could phone Sydney. She was going to be so worried. Grant had to talk to her.

"I have my phone right here. What number do you want me to dial?" David looked into the backseat and saw two children and a young man in the front seat. Nothing made David more angry than guys who thought it was okay to push the limits and run red lights.

"638-9038, it's my wife's phone"

"I can phone your wife after the ambulance arrives and let her know what happened ." David thought it would be easier on the wife if he told her after instead of talking to her husband and having him go unconscious while they were talking.

"No. . .please, I have to talk to her. . .I have to tell her I love her. . .please."

David heard the desperation in his voice and dialed the number. He listened to it ring and when he heard it pick up, he placed the phone to Grant's ear. "Talk," he whispered

"Syd . . . Syd . . . is that you?" Grant found it hard to concentrate and the world was slowly going black.

"Yes, it's me. Grant, is that you? What's wrong?"

"Syd . . . Syd . . ." Grant struggled to get the words out but knew he couldn't give in to the darkness until he told her.

"Grant . . . Grant, are you there? What's happened?"

"Syd . . . I . . . love . . . you," Grant managed before slipping into the darkness, all the while praying that God would take care of his wife.

CHAPTER EIGHT

"**G**rant . . .Grant . . .are you there? Where are you, Grant? What's happened?" Sydney slowly sank to the floor in the entry way of Maria's home. Sydney felt like a heavy weight was on her chest and she was having a hard time breathing. The phone hung limply at her side and there was a voice calling for "Mrs. Gillman" on the other end.

Maria watched in horror as Sydney reacted to what was happening on the other end of the phone. Grabbing the phone from Sydney, Maria answered it.

"Hello . . . "

"Hello, Mrs. Gillman?"

"No, this is her friend, Maria Bennett. Is Grant there? And who are you?"

"My name is David O'Reilly. I'm a paramedic and I was behind Mr. Gillman when he was involved in an accident. Is Mrs. Gillman okay?" David was wishing that the ambulance was already here and that he hadn't let Grant phone his wife. Grant had been so insistent that he didn't have the heart to tell him that it would only make it harder for his wife.

"Mr. O'Reilly . . .were the children with Grant?" The awareness of what had just happened was starting to settle in on Maria and her heart ached for her dear friend. *Dear Lord, please get Syd through this and may your hand of comfort be there, whatever happens from this moment forth.*

"Mrs. Bennett, call me David, and yes there are three children in the vehicle with him. I hear the ambulance and the police have just arrived. I need to tell them what has happened. Mrs. Bennet, you had better get Mrs. Gillman to Spring Hills General Hospital. That's where they'll take them all. I'll come to the hospital as soon as I have everything cleared up here. I was a witness so they will need my statement." David saw that Randy Moorehead was on his way to the truck and was relieved because Randy was one of the best paramedics on the service. In fact, he had taught David everything that he knew. "Randy, over here. One adult male and Randy, there are three children."

"Mrs. Bennett, I have to go now, I'm sorry."

"David, take care of them—they are very special to a lot of people and may God give you the strength and wisdom to do your job. Thank you, David." Maria hung up the phone and looked to where Sydney was sitting and her heart broke. Maria longed to take away the pain that was tearing her friend apart. Sydney struggled with sobs as Maria bent over to help her stand.

"Syd . . .I'm so sorry but we have to get you to the hospital. David said that the ambulance would take Grant and the kids to Spring Hills General."

"Who's David? And what has happened to Grant and the kids?" Sydney struggled to understand what Maria was saying. Everything was so fuzzy and she felt like this was a dream. "Maria, am I dreaming? Surely this has to be a dream."

"No sweetie, this isn't a dream. I wish so much that it was. David was the paramedic that came on the phone after you talked to Grant. Syd, Grant and the kids were in an accident." Maria wasn't sure how she was going to get Sydney to the hospital when she was struggling to keep going with this tragic news. "Syd honey, sit here on the couch while I get my purse and keys."

"No . . . I have to get home now. This has to be a mistake. Grant and the kids are at home waiting for me. I have to go and have pizza with them." Sydney stood and walked to her purse. Searching for her keys, Sydney tried to talk herself into the fact that this was one horrible mistake.

"Syd . . . you know that this is not a dream and you are not driving. I'll take you to the hospital and we'll just take things one thing at a time. Now go and sit on the couch while I get my keys and phone Barry." Sydney looked like a wounded child as she turned and slowly walked to the couch and sat down. Maria grabbed Sydney's keys from the small table in the hall where she always tossed them and ran up the stairs to her room. Maria dialed Barry's office number and prayed that he was there. The phone rang once . . . twice . . . then three times.

"Hello, Barry Bennett speaking."

"Barry . . . oh Barry it's so horrible." As soon as Maria heard Barry's voice her bravado broke and she started to cry.

"Maria, what's happened?" Barry became immediately concerned and started to try and remember what all his children were doing and where they all were.

"Barry, Sydney is here and we just got a call that Grant and the kids were in an accident." Maria wished that Barry were here with her to hold her and tell her everything was going to be all right.

"No way, when?" Barry felt like someone had just punched him in the stomach. *Lord, not Grant and the kids. Please be with them. Lord...Oh no, poor Syd. Father, uphold her at this time.*

"Just now. Barry I have to take Syd to Spring Hills General. Could you meet us there? And phone Pastor Steve and have him put this on the prayer chain." Maria found the courage to carry on in her husband's voice and knew that her friend was going to need her more than ever now.

"Of course. I'll leave now and phone Steve from my cell phone. Maria, God is with you and Syd and He will get us all through this. I'll be praying all the way to the hospital. I'll meet you guys there." Barry jotted a note to give to the assistant coach and packed his briefcase as he talked. Barry just couldn't believe this had happened. Seeing Connor the assistant coach pass his office, he waved for him to come in.

"Barry, I love you and will see you at the hospital. Barry, please be careful."

"I love you too, and Maria, you be careful too. I will be there as soon as I can." Barry hung up the phone and filled Connor in on what had happened. Barry hurried to his car and dialed Pastor Steve.

"Hope Christian Church, Pastor Steve Ironside."

"Pastor Steve, this is Barry."

"Barry, how are things going?"

"Pastor Steve, there's been an accident. Grant and the kids have been involved."

"Grant Gillman? I can't believe it. He was just here this morning. You say the kids were with him. Are they okay? What happened?" Pastor Steve couldn't believe this. He had just been praying with Grant this morning.

"I don't know any details except that Sydney was at our house when she got the call. Maria is taking her to the general hospital and I am going to meet them there. Maria wanted you to put this on the prayer chain." Barry reached his car and unlocked the door. Throwing his briefcase into the backseat he sat down and was struck with the thought that Grant had gotten into his truck just like this and never thought that he would be involved in an accident. Barry was struck anew with how brief and uncertain life could be.

"Barry, I'll phone Dorothy Hamilton right away and get that on the prayer chain. I will leave the church right away and stop and pick up Anita and we will meet you at the hospital. How is Sydney doing?" Pastor Steve flipped through his Rolodex to find Dorothy's number. Finding it, he pulled the card and wondered if Dorothy's daughter Katherine was on call today.

"Thanks Pastor. Maria never said how Sydney was but I'm assuming not well. I will see you at the hospital. Pray, pastor, please pray." Barry started the car and pulled out of his parking place and headed to the hospital—all the time praying for his wife and her friend.

Maria had gotten Sydney into the car and was headed to the hospital. Sydney just sat on the other side of the car in shock. A strangled sob would escape every now and again but she refused to talk. Maria couldn't think of anything to say so she just prayed all the way to the hospital, a drive that seemed to be lasting an eternity.

David O'Reilly was talking to Detective Banks as the second ambulance left the scene taking the two youngest of the Gillman family. Grant and the older boy had been taken first because of their conditions. David hoped this family was going to be okay.

"So you saw the whole thing?" Detective Banks asked. When he arrived on the scene he guessed what had happened and was deeply disturbed when he learned that the victims had included three children.

"Like I said, the gravel truck started to slow but then sped up like he thought that he could make the light. There was nothing that Mr. Gillman could have done. Detective, this is going to haunt me for quite awhile. Was the driver of the gravel truck hurt?" David wished that he had died but knew that hadn't happened when he saw the driver walking around.

"Apart from some scratches and a few sore muscles, no, he wasn't hurt. The driver says that his light was still green and that Mr. Gillman proceeded on a red light. Did you see the light?"

Detective Banks had deliberately saved David until last. He knew that David was helping with the family and that he was in the vehicle behind the Gillman's truck. From all the other witnesses Detective Banks knew that it was the gravel truck that had run the red light but he wanted to hear David's account.

"Are you kidding me? Of course I saw the light and it was green. I was right behind them and was going across the intersection too. If they hadn't been in front of me, I would have been the one he hit. Tell me you don't believe him?" David was angry that this guy had tried to blame Grant Gillman.

"No, I don't believe him. All the other witnesses have collaborated your story. Besides, I ran the driver's name and he has a record. Apparently he has run a red light before and caused an accident. The other driver wasn't hurt but our guy received a warning from his boss. I think our driver will be jobless, in addition to facing charges for this accident. Are you going to be okay, Mr.O'Reilly?"

"Yeah, I'll get over this eventually, it just really bothers me when these guys run the lights and people get hurt. I have to go to the hospital and see how the family is doing. Is there anything else you need from me, Detective?"

"No, that is all. You said that the family knows because the father phoned his wife?"

"Yes, he was insistent that he talk to her and then I talked to a friend, a Mrs. Bennett, and she was going to take the wife to Spring Hills General."

"I will stop by the hospital after I finish here and see how they are doing. Thank you for your help and I am sure they will appreciate all you did for that family. Take care and I will see you later." With that Detective Banks headed in the direction of the gravel truck driver and David headed back to his car and then to the hospital.

CHAPTER NINE

Sydney rode silently in the car beside Maria, being quietly thankful that Maria didn't expect her to talk. Sydney couldn't believe that she was on her way to the hospital. What had troubled her in fitful sleep had in turn become her reality but now she would see four caskets instead of three. Sydney believed that they were all dead because she believed that God had finally exacted his vengeance upon her for her happy, perfect life. Christians are not supposed to have lives filled with happiness, were they? They are supposed to suffer, and now it was her turn. Sydney hoped God was satisfied with Himself because at this moment, she felt as though life were no longer worth living. Everyone that she had ever loved had died. Why couldn't God just leave her alone?

Sydney remembered how as a child she would walk to her Grandma Ruth's house and have tea. Grandma Ruth always had time for Sydney no matter how busy she was. Closing her eyes, Sydney could once again picture herself in the kitchen of Grandma Ruth's home. The kitchen always smelled like fresh bread or cookies; an old radio on the fridge was always on and the coffee was always ready.

Sydney loved the smell of Grandma Ruth's kitchen. It made her feel safe and like nothing bad would ever happen to her. When Sydney was with Grandma Ruth, all the fear in her life disappeared and she experienced a freedom that she felt nowhere else.

"Sydney-Bear, how is my girl today? Come sit and I will make you something to drink. I made cookies today. Your favorite—chocolate chip and oatmeal! Sit Sydney-Bear and we will have a game of checkers. Maybe today you will beat me." Grandma Ruth was a slender woman who looked nowhere near her sixty years. Ruth's hair had started to grey early but with her rich, dark-brown natural color, she looked more elegant than old. Ruth had lived alone in the small town of Tilson for as long as Sydney could remember. Sydney had questioned Grandma Ruth about where Grandpa was but she never talked about him. There were no pictures and Sydney's mom refused to talk about her father. This had left Sydney wondering about this mysterious man and what he could have done so that nobody would mention his name. She would imagine that he was some kind of spy on a secret mission that people were forbidden to speak of. She had a vivid imagination and there were a great many scenarios that passed through her mind as to the reason why no one would talk about Grandpa Stern.

"Grandma, can I have coffee today?" Sydney loved the smell of the coffee even as a child and would always ask to see if this would finally be the day that she was old enough to try some of the aromatic, dark brew.

"Sydney-Bear, why do you want coffee? You are too young and it will only stunt your growth. I have some milk that will taste so good with the warm cookies."

"But Grandma, I am almost eleven years old. Please, may I have some coffee? I will put milk and sugar in it so it is not so strong. Just half a cup, please Grandma?" Sydney looked at her Grandma with that endearing gaze that she knew Grandma could never say no to.

"Sydney-Bear, you are going to get me into trouble with your mother. Only a quarter of a cup and you have to fill the rest of the cup up with milk. Promise?" Ruth loved it when Sydney came to visit and she really had a hard time saying no to her first grandchild. Ruth adored all of her grandchildren but Sydney was the only one who came and spent a great deal of time with her. Ruth thought that Sydney would move in if she was allowed but Ruth knew that would never be permitted. Cynthia had been very clear on how much time her children would be allowed to spend with their grandmother until Ruth sought out some medical help. The nerve of Cynthia, telling her that she needed to see some shrink. Ruth knew that some days she was a little depressed but it wasn't like she needed help. It just infuriated her when she thought about it so she worked at putting it out of her mind and instead concentrated on enjoying the time with her granddaughter.

"Oh, Grandma, I promise! *THANK YOU*. You are the best Grandma in the whole world. I have to be home before five, Mom said, but don't know why. I have no homework and its Kirby's day to do dishes so I wouldn't be missed. Grandma, can I stay longer, please? Could you phone Mom and get her to let me stay?" Sydney loved to be at Grandma's and knew her feeling of security would vanish when she left this house. Sydney longed to stay with Grandma always and had even brought it up to her parents. That had not gone well, to say the least. Her mother had about hit the fan and ranted and raved about it for days. Needless to say, Sydney's visits had been limited and there were no overnight stays anymore. Sydney knew her mother loved Grandma Ruth but there was something that Sydney didn't know that caused her mother to worry every time they visited. Sydney only hoped that one day she would understand so that she could spend more time with Grandma Ruth.

"Sydney-Bear, you know that your Mother wants you home and it would only make her upset if we try to change the rules. Don't worry about it and let's just enjoy this time that we have. Here are some cookies and here, my dear, is your quarter cup of coffee." Ruth set the cookies and the mug in front of Sydney before pouring one for herself. Sitting down across the table from Sydney, Ruth took a cookie and asked, "So, Sydney-Bear, how was your day at school?"

Sydney proceeded to explain how Anthony Birk annoyed her to death and was always pulling her hair or tackling her or pushing her into her locker. She shared all about her friend Darlene and how they were going to work on a special project for extra credit in social studies class. Ruth listened as Sydney talked about her day, but all the while she was growing weary and she could sense the darkness gathering around her. The despair was taking root and she knew that soon she would need to ask Sydney to leave, because coping with life would quickly become impossible. Ruth knew that these "moods" as she called them, would pass but they were something that she knew she didn't want her granddaughter to see. The heaviness began to descend and Ruth found it harder and harder to concentrate on what Sydney had to say. *God, help me through this, please just a little longer to spend with Sydney. I get so little time with her. Please hold back the darkness. Just a little more time.*

"Grandma, are you listening to me?" Sydney saw the change in her Grandma and wondered if it was time to leave. Sydney had seen this change before, where Grandma's happiness soon melted into unhappiness, and then she was no longer the fun-loving Grandma Sidney adored. "It's about time for me to go. Thank you for the cookies and coffee. I will see you on Friday on my way home from school. Are you going to be okay, Grandma?"

"Oh, Sydney-Bear, I will be okay. You be safe on the way home now and I will make a cake for you on Friday. Grandma loves you, Sydney-Bear, please don't ever forget how much I love you and how much Jesus loves you. Promise me, Sydney-Bear, please promise me, you won't forget?"

"I promise, Grandma, and I love you too." With that, Sydney left and walked the short distance home, wondering why Grandma had been so insistent that she remember how much she loved her.

As Sydney sat in Maria's car it dawned on her that was the last time she had seen Grandma Ruth alive. Why would she remember that now? Later that night, after Sydney had gone to bed, she remembered that the phone had rung and woken up her parents. Sydney lay there and listened to what was happening in the next room.

"Cynthia, you had better get dressed. Your mother is in trouble again. That was Bernard and he has already called the police. At least he called us too, this time, but I think we had better get there before the police do. Cynthia, she needs help. You need to put your foot down. We can't keep doing this." Chett put his shirt on and grabbed his socks while Cynthia hurriedly dressed.

"Chett, unless she wants to get help it is no use to talk to her. You know I've tried. We better hurry. How long ago did Bernard phone the police?" Cynthia dreaded what would surely happen next and prayed that somehow, this would be the time her mother would seek help before it was too late.

"Just before he called us, so maybe we will get there in time. He never said what happened but told me it wasn't good and that we had better hurry."

"I'm ready, let's go. Pray Chett, that's all we can do now. I hope she hasn't hurt herself this time." Cynthia followed Chett out the door and left Sydney to wonder what was happening at Grandma Ruth's house that required the police. Sydney lay awake hoping to wait for her parents to get home but she soon drifted back to sleep and woke the next morning to find that her parents were still not home.

Sydney found Maria asleep on the couch and knew that her parents had probably called her so that Sydney, Kirby and Chad wouldn't be alone.

"Maria, where are my parents?"

"What? Oh, Syd…wow, I was really sleeping. Your mom phoned me last night from the hospital and asked me to come over and get you all off to school. I think your Grandma is in the hospital, although my Mom knows more than I do." Maria was never an early riser but she had been glad to come when she heard something had happened to Sydney's Grandma. Maria knew how close they were and wanted to help in any way that she could. Maria had come home for the week because Barry was in the middle of exams and she was a "nuisance," as he put it, when he was trying to study. Besides, Jesse loved to visit her Grandparents and Maria could use the extra sleep now that she was expecting their second child. It seemed like all she could do for those first three months had been to sleep and feel nauseated. But this too would pass, she kept telling herself. Just a few more weeks and then she would be past the first trimester and would finally feel better.

"Maria, what happened to my Grandma?" Sydney felt fear as her imagination began to take control and many horrible things began to play out in her mind.

"Syd, I don't know. All they said was that they were at the hospital with her." Maria saw the fear in Sydney's eyes and wished that she had more answers to calm the fear. "Sydney, don't worry, I'm sure they will phone before you go to school to tell you what happened. Now let's get your brother and sister up and get some breakfast made."

"Grandma Ruth is dead." Sydney didn't know how or why but she just knew that she would never see her Grandma again.

"No, we don't know that, Syd. Let's just wait until we hear from your parents." It scared Maria how certain Sydney seemed to be and silently prayed that the girl was wrong.

"I know it. My Grandma Ruth is dead."

"Syd, let's pray for your Grandma right now." Maria knew of nothing else to do except pray and hoped that it would comfort Sydney and take away the fear and anxiety about her grandma being in the hospital.

"Will it help, Maria, will God listen to me?" Sydney had asked God to forgive her of her sins and come into her heart at camp last summer but she had never felt Him and wondered if He was really there.

"Of course God will listen to you. You love God and He loves you. Remember, Syd, what you learned at camp last summer? God is always there for you. Let's pray and ask Him to keep your Grandma safe and to help you to not to be afraid." Maria knelt by the sofa and pulled Sydney down beside her. "You pray first and then I will pray after you. Okay, Syd?"

"Okay. Dear God, this is Sydney and I asked you to come into my heart last summer but I'm not sure you are there. But anyway, could you please keep my Grandma safe? She is the best Grandma ever and I really love her. God, please don't let her die. Help me to know you are here and to not worry. Amen."

Maria's heart broke as she listened to Sydney pray and knew that she would need to lift Sydney up in prayer and try to keep in contact with her to help her know how much God loved her.

"Dear Lord, thank you for being here with us even when we don't feel you. Thank you for your love and right now, be with Grandma Ruth and keep her in your hand and, if it's your will, heal her. Lord, be with Cynthia and Chett at the hospital and with Sydney here at home. Help them to not worry and to trust you in everything. Thank you for all that you do and be with Barry during his exams. Keep him safe. I love you, Lord. Amen."

Just then Sydney's parents walked through the door.

Cynthia was crying and ran straight to her bedroom, closing the door behind her. Chett was very solemn and sat down at the kitchen table, looking like he had the weight of the world on his shoulders. Sydney got up from beside the sofa and ran to her father, wrapping her arms around his neck while he lifted her onto his lap.

"Daddy, is Grandma Ruth okay?" Sydney burrowed her face into his shirt with fear about what he was going to say. Deep down, she knew the answer, and was terrified that he would confirm her worst fears.

"Sydney, Grandma Ruth is in the hospital and we don't know how long she will be there." Chett knew that Sydney would not understand that Ruth had tried to take her own life and they had decided that it was best that the children did not know that detail—at least for now. Chett hated the fact that he was the one who had insisted that they keep her for longer than just a couple of days, but…Ruth needed help and maybe this was the only way to get it for her. Ruth had cried and pleaded for them to take her home, giving her word that she would never try to do this again. But Chett had heard it all before. The sight of her lying there in the yard with one wrist slit and trying to slit the other was one that would haunt him for a very long time.

"Daddy, can I go see Grandma?" Sydney was relieved that Grandma was not dead and now wanted to see her more than ever. Grandma had to know how much Sydney loved her so she could get better and come home.

"Sydney, the rules at the hospital where Grandma is won't let you in to see her. But as soon as she is out, we will visit her. I can give her a message for you if you want. Your mother and I have to go back after lunch so write out your note and I will take it to her."

"But a note is not the same. Please, can you get me in to see her? Please, Daddy?" Sydney was suddenly desperate to see Grandma as though if she didn't now, she would never again get the chance.

"Sydney, I can't. It's the rule. Go get ready for school and I will drive all of you today." Chett was just too weary to argue the point more and yet he knew that this whole ordeal was not going to be easy on either Cynthia or the children.

Sydney had slowly made her way to her room and gotten dressed and ready for school. The last thing that she wanted to do was go to school but she knew that her parents would never allow her to miss the day. Maria had said that she would keep praying for Grandma Ruth and for Sydney when she left, but that did little to calm Sydney's fears. As Chett drove them to school Sydney wondered why she couldn't feel God. Was He really there or not? Maybe something was wrong with her and that was why she couldn't feel Him. Oh well, it didn't matter as long as He kept her Grandma safe. That was the most important thing of all.

The school day had been one of the longest days ever for Sydney and when the bus finally dropped them off at home, she was relived to see her parent's car at home. As she walked up the driveway, Sydney also noticed that Maria's parents car and the pastor's car were parked out front as well. Sydney rushed to the house and burst through the door to the kitchen and found her mother crying.

"Mom, what's wrong? Is Grandma okay?" Sydney's chest felt heavy as she looked around the room and saw looks of sympathy on all the faces. Maria walked up to Sydney and drew her into a warm embrace.

"Syd," Maria whispered, "your Grandma is no longer in the hospital. She died and went to heaven." Maria felt Sydney stiffen and then collapse against her as the sobs came.

"But we prayed for her! Did God not hear? Why, Maria? Why didn't He hear me?" Sydney sank into the grief that overtook her and knew from that moment on she would never forgive God for letting her Grandma Ruth die. For some reason God hated her. Maybe it was because she couldn't feel him. On that day, Sydney vowed that she would live the rest of her life trying to be good so that God would never want to punish her again by taking away the people she loved the most.

CHAPTER TEN

Sydney had from that moment lived a life that on the outside anyway, appeared to be the perfect Christian example. Sydney went to church, attended all the young peoples events, taught Sunday School, attended Bible studies, was on numerous church committees, excelled in all her school studies and in sports but even still, she felt her life was empty and the fears started to entwine themselves into every area of her life until she thought she was going to go crazy. All through high school she struggled to hide her fear that she wasn't going to be good enough and God would punish her again. When Sydney had finally found out that her Grandma Ruth had attempted to commit suicide and then had been successful in the hospital, she struggled with the thoughts that she was more like her Grandma then she wanted to be. Surely Grandma's breakdown was hereditary and Sydney was slowly going crazy too.

Sydney had done a fine job of hiding her real feelings and had put aside the thoughts that she was crazy when she had met and married Grant. Life was perfect until that fateful day when Sydney received the phone call. Sydney was home with six-month old Brendan when the phone had rung. Grant had just walk through the door for lunch as Sydney answered the phone.

"Hello."

"Hello, is this Mrs. Sydney Gillman?"

"Yes, this is she." Sydney wondered about the authority and dread in the voice on the other end of the line. Something inside her told her this was not good news. Seeing Grant walk through the door she knew that he was alright. Quietly Sydney asked, *"What now God?"*

"Mrs. Gillman, this is detective Bryan Corban from the Sedona police department. I tried to get in touch with your parents but there was no answer. Do you know where they are, Mrs. Gillman?" Bryan Corban loved his job but hated this part and wished that he had better news for the family.

Sydney now knew that something had happened and her chest felt like a heavy weight was on it and she was starting to have a hard time breathing. Trying to concentrate, she whispered, "My parents have gone to the cabin for the weekend and won't be home until Monday. Why do you want to talk to them?" Sydney braced herself for the blow she knew was going to come.

"Mrs. Gillman , I am sorry to have to tell you this but there has been an accident. Hans and Esther Forrester were hit head-on in an automobile accident early this morning. I am sorry but they were both killed instantly. They never suffered at all." Bryan knew that this would be a blow, especially losing both grandparents at the same time. Nothing made Bryan's blood boil more than drunk drivers that killed someone, especially when they walked away with out a scratch.

Sydney heard him say they were both killed and the room started to spin; she couldn't catch her breath. Slowly she sunk to the ground and dropped the phone. Grant ran across the room and quickly picked up the phone as he sat next to his wife and drew her into his arms.

"Hello, this is Grant Gillman. Who is this?"

"Hello, Mr. Gillman, this is Detective Bryan Corban with the Sedona Police Department. Is Mrs. Gillman okay?" Bryan was instantly relieved that Mrs. Gillman was not alone but still hated that he had to be the bearer of bad news.

"Detective, my wife appears to have heard some upsetting news. Would you please tell me what you told her?" Grant dreaded the news that would cause this reaction in his wife and tried to prepare himself.

"Mr. Gillman , I am sorry to have to tell you this and I really did not want to tell your wife but I couldn't get a hold of Mr. and Mrs. Forrester and Mrs. Gillman was next on the list. I am really very sorry but Hans and Esther Forrester were in a head-on collision this morning and were both killed instantly. Mr. Gillman, we need to get in touch with Mr. Chett Forrester as soon as possible."

Bryan felt for the family but knew that arrangements had to be made and the bodies identified as soon as possible.

"Detective, did they suffer and how did this happen?" Grant felt as though he had been punched in the stomach. He couldn't believe that they were both gone. Hans and Esther had been like his own grandparents.

"No sir, they did not suffer and it was a drunk driver that crossed the center line and hit them. They were not at fault. We have the other driver in custody and charges are being laid as we speak. Mr. Gillman, is there a way to get in touch with Mr. Forrester?"

"Yes, I have the cell phone number and will call them right away. Can I get your number and your name again so that they can call you?" Grant reached over to the coffee table and grabbed the pen and paper. Writing down all the information, Grant told the detective he would call back as soon as he reached his in-laws. Hanging up the phone, Grant pulled Sydney closer and the two of them wept for the tragic loss of two wonderful people.

Maria and the children had come over as soon as they heard about the accident. Jesse kept Brendan busy and out of trouble. Jesse had been thrilled when Brendan was born and carried him around whenever she was there or when they were at church. Brendan loved the attention from Jesse and smiled whenever she was around. Maria made a pot of coffee and sat Sydney down at the table. Sydney was quiet and although the tears had stopped, they were just under the surface and ready to spill forth at any moment.

"Sydney, Grant told me all the details. Has he been able to get in touch with your parents?" Maria feared what this would do to Sydney. She remembered all too clearly when Ruth had died and the change that had taken place in Sydney. Although Maria lived in Spring Hills, she had kept in touch with Sydney and tried to encourage her. Maria knew that Sydney blamed God for Ruth's death and feared that this might turn Sydney completely away from God.

"Yes, he was able to get through to Mom and Dad almost immediately. They should be home in a couple of hours. Dad is going to fly to Sedona tonight and Mom will stay here and start the arrangements. Dad's two sisters will arrive at ten tomorrow morning and Grant is going to meet them at the airport. Their families will drive out closer to the funeral." Sydney was spent; she had no energy left. Sitting here with Maria was an effort but she was glad that her best friend was here. Maria had been there the day Grandma Ruth had died and now here she was again. Sydney would never ever be able to repay her for her support and comfort.

"Sydney, I know you are grieving but are you...I mean... have you prayed about this?" Maria wasn't sure if this was the time but she knew that the old fears were surfacing for she could see them in Sydney's eyes.

"Maria, does God hate me? Is He doing this to me because I can't feel Him? I just don't understand. I have tried to be good and still He takes away the people I love.

And no, I haven't prayed. Why should I? He's not listening anyway." Sydney couldn't believe that this was happening again. First Grandma Ruth and now both of her grandparents on her father's side. What had she done to warrant this?

"Syd, God doesn't hate you. He loves you more than you could ever know. Syd, you don't have to feel Him for Him to be here and He always listens to your prayer. Syd, I know that this is hard but don't doubt God's love for you. Cling to Him and He will help you through this." Maria had been afraid something like this would happen but she wasn't sure how to handle it. *God, please give me the words for Syd. She needs you more now then ever and yet she seems to be running from You. Help me to help her, Lord.*

Sydney had heard it all before and although she had opened the door to this topic, she was not up to talking about it now.

"Maria, let's not talk about this now. I have way too much to do and Mom is going to need my help to plan the funeral. The coffee is done. Would you like a cup?"

Maria stood up knowing that she had been shut down trying to help her friend.

"Sure, but let me get it. Just try to relax. I'm sure the next few days are going to be trying." Maria grabbed a couple of mugs and filled them with coffee. Placing one in front of Sydney she asked " Syd, would you like Jesse to stay here and help take care of Brendan for the next few days?"

"Yeah, that would sure help. Thanks, Maria." Sydney knew that Maria only meant well when she told her that God loved her but it didn't help. Sydney was starting to wonder if she should believe in a God who let bad things happen. It was so hard to understand why He didn't stop these bad things from happening when He had the power to do so. It wasn't fair that her grandparents who were good people and loved God had to die and some drunk was allowed to live.

Sydney was angry and there was nothing that anyone could say that was going to change her mind.

Jesse turned out to be a real help over the next few days. She looked after Brendan and helped reheat the casseroles brought over by the church ladies. When someone came to drop off some baking or casseroles Sydney always happened to be busy and Jesse answered the door. Sydney just couldn't bear hearing their mindless chatter and sympathies. They didn't understand how she felt and the last thing she needed was their pious cliches such as "this will work out for good for those who love God" or "they are in a better place," "we know how you feel," and especially "God rejoices at the death at one of His saints" Apparently, that was in the Bible someplace. How could God rejoice at the death of her grandparents when everyone else was grieving?

Sydney made it through the next few days on little sleep and even less food. Grant had taken two weeks off and was always there supporting her. His comfort had meant so much and she was sure she wouldn't have gotten through it without him. When the day of the funeral arrived, it was all Sydney could do to get out of bed and get ready. She dreaded the funeral and all the supposed answers that all the people would have and the pastor's "words of comfort." Did he really think that telling the family that this was God's will was going to comfort them? Why couldn't people just quit trying to fix the emotions of a family tragedy and let the family grieve? That is all Sydney wanted—just to be left alone.

Grant had come into the bedroom to see if Sydney was awake and found her sitting on the side of the bed crying. Sitting next to her, he drew her into his arms and held her. Grant was worried about her and had spent a lot of time praying for her the last few days. Maria had told Grant about their talk and Grant had tried to talk to Sydney but she didn't want to talk about God at all. So Grant did the only thing that he knew to do—he prayed.

"Syd, you need to get ready. I know you don't want to go but you need to. It will help you to gain some closure in this. You need to be around your family and they need you." Grant's heart broke seeing his wife so broken with grief and running from God.

"Grant, I just don't know if I can do this. It is so hard." Sydney buried her face into Grant's, sobbing.

"Syd, I know how hard this is but I will be there with you and God will be there with you also." Grant hoped that in some way this would help her in her time of need. Grant just didn't know what to say to help her so he opted to just hold her and be there for her.

Slowly Sydney's sobs subsided and she rose from the bed to get herself ready. She knew she had to go and only hoped that she could hold it all together and just get through the day. At the funeral Pastor Blackley had spoken about how Hans and Esther were in a much better place and how much they had loved God. He then went on to say how much Hans and Esther would want everyone there to accept Jesus as their personal Lord and Savior so that they would see them some day in heaven. Sydney wondered why anyone would want to believe in a God who let bad things happen? At that moment Sydney knew that she could never trust God. She would continue to live the "Christian life" but only for Grant and Maria's sakes. God meant so much to them that she couldn't let them down but for herself, there was no hope left that God loved her. She vowed that from this day forward Grant and her family would be her life and she would do everything in her power to keep them safe.

It was shortly after the funeral that the nightmares started. Over and over Sydney dreamed about the caskets and as each child was born one more casket was added to the funeral. Sydney lay awake many nights planning the funerals because she believed that eventually she would be required to put those plans into action.

That time had now come. Sydney sat in Maria's car riding slowly to the hospital where she would find out that her funeral plans were now needed. *How would she go on? Life was no longer worth living.* At that moment Maria drove into the parking lot of Spring Hills General Hospital. Sydney got ready to get out of the car. Looking at the front doors of the emergency room she murmured to herself, "and so it begins."

CHAPTER ELEVEN

Maria watched as Sydney slowly got out of the car. Standing beside the front bumper, it looked like Sydney was frozen to that spot, terrified to take another step towards the hospital. Maria grabbed her purse and threw her keys in the front pocket as she shouldered the bag. Heading towards Sydney, Maria prayed. *Lord , help me to know what to say. Please help Grant and the children to be okay and please, please God, help Sydney to turn to You and not completely abandon You. God, please help me.*

Sydney turned and the look in her eyes caused Maria's heart to once again be torn in two for her friend. Reaching over to where Sydney stood, Maria hugged her, letting Sydney know how much she was loved and that she was not alone no matter what the outcome. Just then an ambulance rolled up to the emergency room doors with lights flashing and sirens blaring. The back door burst open as the driver jumped from the side and sprinted to the back to help unload the patients. Grabbing the stretcher, he pulled it out until the legs fell into place. Another paramedic followed the stretcher out, holding the IV bag that was attached to the small, blood-covered patient on the stretcher. A large, male ER nurse ran out of the hospital and Sydney stared in disbelief as she heard him ask, "Are these the last two from the accident on Twenty-sixth Avenue? There were only four right?"

Sydney caught her breath as the paramedic answered, "Yes. Jason, help Jack with this one and send someone else out to help me with the boy. Any word how the dad and the other boy are?"

"I haven't heard anything. They're both upstairs, one for x-rays and another for a CAT scan. Randy was the one that brought them both in and he filled me in on what happened." Jason Turner had been a nurse for ten years and had witnessed many tragedies, but when they involved children, even after all these years, it was still hard for him to take.

"You would not believe the truck, totaled I'm sure, and the other driver didn't have so much as a scratch. I looked him over myself. But was I ever ready to inflict some of my own wounds on him." Jack Kennedy had just arrived for his shift when the call had come in. A twenty-year veteran, he had seen it all, but after today he was seriously considering finding another profession.

Maria and Sydney witnessed the exchange between the nurse and the paramedics. Suddenly Maria felt Sydney begin to slowly crumple. Maria struggled to hold on to Sydney and keep her from falling to the ground.

"Syd. . .Please, let's go inside, it's going to be okay. Can someone help me, please " Maria knew from what they had just seen that the reality of it all was beginning to sink in for Sydney.

As a small female nurse came out of the ER doors, the paramedic in the ambulance pointed to Maria in the parking lot who was struggling to hold Sydney up. "Go help them and I'll wait for Jack to come back. From the looks of that lady you had better take a wheelchair with you."

Realizing that the paramedic was motioning towards her as the one that needed help, Sydney slowly rose to her feet clinging to Maria and whispered, "Maria, tell them to help the child in the ambulance, that's more important." Feeling like there was a great burden on her shoulders, Sydney looked to the ambulance and spoke aloud what both were thinking. " It's one of my boys and the other small patient with the IV was. . .was my Sarah Rose ."

Maria helped Sydney to her feet and made sure she was stable as she yelled to the approaching nurse, "It's okay, just take care of the boy. He needs you more than we do. We will be in shortly."

Making sure the one woman was standing on her own, the ER nurse turned back to help move the next patient from inside of the ambulance into the hospital. Leaning into the ambulance she grabbed the stretcher and pulled. When the legs dropped into place, the paramedic jumped out and they rushed towards the ER doors.

Sydney watched as the stretcher was pulled under the entrance lights and tried to see which of her boys lay so still and quiet. Slowly moving closer to the doors, she caught a glimpse of matted, brown, curly hair and realized it was Scott.

"Maria, it's Scotty." Sydney picked up the pace and was in a full run by the time she reached the doors to the hospital. Maria reached the doors in time to see Sydney yell Scotty's name and collapse on to the floor, sobbing. Rushing through the doors and kneeling beside Sydney, Maria looked around for some help just as the nurse from behind the desk rushed over to them and asked if they were okay.

"No, we are not okay," Maria replied, she hadn't meant to be so abrupt but what a stupid question to ask after what she just saw. Surely she could tell that something was wrong. "This is Mrs. Gillman and she was told that her husband and three children were being brought here."

Maria watched as the realization of who Sydney was dawned on the nurse and immediately saw the sympathy in her eyes. She directed them to a private waiting room and told them she would go and tell the doctor that they were here. As the nurse closed the door, she looked again at Sydney, who was sobbing in the corner chair and mouthed the words "I'm sorry" to Maria.

Maria held Sydney's hand while she rifled through her purse to find some Kleenex. Finding only two tissues in her purse Maria knew that this was going to be sadly insufficient for the hours ahead. Handing them to Sydney she struggled with her own tears and wondered how long it would take Barry and Pastor Steve to get there.

"Maria. . .did. . .did you see Scotty? There was so. . .so much blood, I hardly. . .recognized him." Sydney stared at the floor as she tried to gain some sort of control over her emotions before the doctor came. She couldn't help but wonder how long it would be before they would hear anything and if she would be allowed to see Grant and the kids. That's if they were even still alive. The thought of having to saying good-bye after they had died was just too much for her to bear.

"I saw him, Syd. . .let's try to wait for the doctor before we worry too much." Maria could hear the all the commotion in the hall and the sound of people rushing back and forth. Silently she prayed that God would give the doctors wisdom as they treated her friend's family. Maria shook her head in disbelief as she thought once more about what had happened. It was then that she remembered that Jesse and her husband were coming for supper and they wouldn't know what had happened. Searching through her purse for her cell phone she remembered that she wouldn't be permitted to use it in the hospital anyway and turned it off instead. Looking then for change to use in the pay phone, she asked, "Syd, do you have your cell phone with you? You should turn it off. We can't have them on in the hospital."

Checking her coat pockets, Sydney realized that she

didn't even have her purse with her. "No, I don't know where it is. I think you were the last one to talk on it."

"That's right, now I remember, it's on my night table. I put it there when I phoned Barry." The door to the waiting room squeaked as it opened and both ladies jumped as they looked to see who was coming through the door. Each was wondering if there was already news and if it would be good news. Opening the door was the nurse who had escorted them to this waiting room holding two blankets and she was talking to someone in the hall.

"They are in here, sir, and will there be any other family coming that I should show in here?" Holding the door, she stood back as Barry enter the room with Pastor Steve and Anita close behind. Pastor Steve walked directly to Sydney and sat in the chair next to her and Anita followed, and as she passed Maria, she squeezed her shoulder and then sat in the chair next to her husband. Barry continued to talk to the nurse, telling her that more family would be coming in over the next few hours and that she should make sure they knew where Sydney was. The nurse gave Barry the blankets, explaining they were for Maria and Sydney, she then quietly left. As the door closed Barry slipped a blanket around Sydney's shoulders and turning to Maria, he sat in the seat next to his wife, drawing her into his embrace, wrapping the second blanket around her and asked, "Has there been any news?"

"No, nothing yet. We haven't been here that long." Maria felt Barry's strength and was relieved that he was here. "The ambulance with Scott and Sarah Rose arrived just after we did and Sydney saw them. This is going to be really hard and she's going to need us more than ever now. Oh, I forgot I need to phone Jesse. They were supposed to come for supper tonight." Maria started to rise but Barry held her in place.

"It's okay, Maria, I phoned Jesse on my here. She was

going to phone the other kids and volunteered to phone Syd's parents to let them know. She's going to let Cynthia take care of letting the rest of the family know. I wouldn't be surprised to see more family show up within the next hour. I hope we have some news for them." Barry still couldn't believe this was happening. Looking over at Sydney, his heart broke at the sight of her fear and how broken she looked.

Pastor Steve and Anita had prayed all the way to the hospital for the Gillman family. But now that they were here and saw the fear in Sydney's eyes there were no words they could say to console her. How do you comfort someone who is running from God and may turn completely away from Him because of this tragedy? Steve and Anita had talked about the change in Sydney and had both sensed that she was struggling but would never talk about it. They had prayed for her many times. On the way to the hospital they had decided that they would just be there for her, love her and help her in any way possible. Anita had told Steve that the last thing Sydney needed now were some Christian clichés and that what she really needed to see was God's love in action. As both of them prayed silently for wisdom in this situation, Anita reached over and grasped Sydney's hand.

"Sydney, I don't know what to say to help you and there is nothing that I can do to fix this but I do want you to know that you are not alone and I will stay here with you as long as you need me to. Steve will be here as often as he can but I will stay here or go and get anything that you need. We love you, Sydney, and want to be here for you."

Sydney didn't know what to say. She had expected them to come in here and start praying for everyone and tell her this was God's will and that everything would work out for good. But she never expected this and she wasn't sure quite how to handle it.

"Thank you. . .and thank you for coming. How did you

find out so fast? I haven't even phoned my family yet."
Sydney suddenly realized that she needed to phone Grant's
parents as well as her own. They needed to know what had
happened. This was her worst nightmare. She was going to
have to phone Bob and Roberta and tell them their son
might be dead. Sydney started to cry as she said, "I need to
phone Grant's. . .Grant's mom and his dad."

"Syd," Barry leaned over so that he could see her face
and continued, "Jesse phoned your parents already and told
them. Cynthia will let the rest of the family know. Don't
worry, we have it all taken care of. Your parents should be
here soon." Barry squeezed Maria's hand and stood up, all
the while hating the feeling of not being able to do something to fix this. "I think that I will go and see if they are
here and ask the nurse if there is any news yet. Pastor, would
you like to come with me?"

"Yes, I'll come with you. Besides, I need to phone Saul
and cancel the board meeting for tonight. I'd forgotten all
about it until now. I'm sure the phone chain has reached
them and they're probably wondering what is happening."
Pastor Steve stood up and headed to the door to join Barry
and Anita, who moved closer to Sydney who was still holding her hand.

"Steve, why don't you bring back some coffee for us all.
It could be a while and if you could find some food I think
we are going to have to keep up our strength." Anita wasn't
sure if Sydney would eat but thought that the distraction
would be good.

"Great idea, any special orders or is black okay with
everyone?" Steve was happy to have something to do. He
had always felt awkward in these situations, never knowing
what to say or do and was thankful for his wife's insightful
wisdom and her level head in times of crisis.

"Black will be just fine. Thank you, Steve." Anita
smiled at him as he turned and joined Barry in the hall.

"I know that you probably don't feel like eating but your hands feel cold and I thought maybe some coffee would warm you up." Anita placed Sydney's hand between her own and started to rub it, trying to warm it a little. Anita had remembered when they had lost their child and how she felt. She could only imagine how much more Sydney suffered with her whole family somewhere within the hospital walls . The unknown must be just about unbearable for her. Silently she prayed, *Lord, give me the actions and the words for Sydney. You know what she is struggling with and the worry for her family. Lord, You are all powerful and love us more than we could ever imagine. Please show Sydney your comfort and peace in this time. And , Lord, if we could hear something soon, please. Thank you for being here with us and never letting us out of the palm of your hand.*

All three women sat in silence waiting for the men to come back with the coffee or else for a doctor with news on the fate of the Gillman family. All of them jumped when once again the door squeaked as it was opened. Sydney slowly looked towards the door wondering if she really wanted to hear how her family was. She just wasn't sure if she could handle it. At this moment she was trying desperately to keep herself together and she knew that if the news was bad...well, thoughts of Grandma Ruth came to her mind and being committed wasn't out of the question. Sydney felt like she was teetering on the brink of losing her mind if she had to go through one more funeral. Sydney immediately recognized the person standing in the doorway. Jumping up, she ran to the warm embrace of her father's arms.

"Oh, Daddy, what am I going to do?" And the tears started anew as she buried her face into Chett Forrester's chest, wishing once again that she was the small girl in her youth, sometime before all the fear and pain of death had entered her life.

CHAPTER TWELVE

Chett and Cynthia Forrester had just arrived at the home of Kirby, their second daughter, to spend a few days before continuing on to Sedona for a brief holiday. When the phone had rung, Kirby had been in the middle of helping her youngest child Cory with an art piece and asked that Chett answer it. Little did he know what message awaited him on the other end. A crying Jesse who was relieved to finally get hold of him, relayed the news of the accident and that everyone was at the hospital. Jesse had no real news on their conditions—all she knew was that Grant and all three children had been involved in the accident and taken to Spring Hills General Hospital. After assuring her that he would let the rest of the family know what had happened, he hung up the phone, and bowing his head, he sent up a brief prayer for Sydney, Grant and the children. After praying for strength, Chett immediately dialed the senior Gillman's home in Phoenix. Thankfully, Bob answered the phone, but hating the fact that he was the bearer of bad news, Chett greeted him and then broke the news of the accident to him. Bob and Roberta said that they would catch the next flight out and would phone Hilary, their daughter, to pick them up when they arrived. Bob asked that Chett phone them as soon as he heard any news whatsoever and gave him their cell phone number. Hanging up the phone, Chett went to find his wife and daughter to share with them the sad news. Chett's heart ached for his oldest daughter and wasn't sure what he would find when he got to the hospital, for he knew how the deaths of her grandparents had affected Sydney.

Chett and Cynthia had driven to the hospital in silence, each praying for their grandchildren, son-in-law and comfort for their daughter. They were thankful that they had left a day early and were already so close to Spring Hills when they had received the news.

Arriving at the hospital they met Barry and Pastor Steve outside the waiting room talking to a paramedic named Randy Moorehead.

"Chett, Cynthia, you are here so soon. You must have really sped from Tilson or should I say flown. By the way, how did you get here so fast?" Barry realized that there was no way they could have driven that distance in less then two hours and it had only been an hour since he had heard the news.

"We had just arrived at Kirby's when Jesse caught up with us. We decided to leave a day early to head down to Sedona and now we're glad that we did." Chett could see in Barry's face the weariness that was the result of the news and the waiting. "Do we know what happened yet? Is there any news on how they are?"

"No, we haven't heard anything about how they are but Mr. Moorehead was at the accident and he was filling us in on what had happened." Barry turned to Randy and said "Randy, this is Chett and Cynthia Forrester, they are Sydney Gillman's parents."

"Nice to meet you both. I am really sorry to have to meet you under these circumstances." Randy was glad that Mrs. Gillman had so many who cared about her and were here for her. He was glad that he had been able to be of some help at the accident and was able to settle some questions for the family. Randy's shift had just ended when they receive the call for the accident. He had decided to go when he heard that David had witnessed the accident and had called it in. Randy had phoned his wife later from the hospital to tell her what had happened and that he would be late. Brenda Moorehead understood her husband's need to know how the children were doing. His compassion for his patients was one of the things that she loved about him the most. She also knew that he wouldn't sleep or eat and would just pace around the house if he came home before he knew something.

Randy continued to fill them in on what he knew and which of their loved ones had been transported first and those who came later. Randy had learned each of their names and was able to shed some light on the accident for the family. He was glad to be able to at least let them know that they had all been alive when they arrived here but that is all he would say about their conditions. Randy secretly feared for the father but did not want to add to their worry on his gut feeling.

"Mr. Moorehead, thank you for sharing what happened. It answers some of the questions." Chett then turned to Barry and asked, "Barry, does Sydney know what happened?"

"No, we just found out now for ourselves what happened. She is in the waiting room right here with Maria and Anita. We were just on our way to see if there was any news and to get some coffee and food. Would you two like anything?" Barry looked towards the nurse's station to see if there was someone for him to talk to.

"Yes, some coffee would be great. Mr. Moorehead, would you consider coming and sharing what happened with our daughter?" Chett knew that Sydney would have more questions than he could answer and Randy would be the best person to answer them for her.

"Yes, I will come and talk to her if you think that is best." Randy knew that it would be far more difficult to tell what he had witnessed to the mother and wife of the victims but also knew that she would have questions that he would be able to answer for her.

"Thank you, and yes I think it would be best if it came from you. Would you like some coffee or something to eat also?" Chett looked towards the waiting room and wondered how his daughter was doing.

"If it's no trouble, a coffee would be great. And if we are lucky, there may be some baking left that is usually pretty good for a hospital cafeteria. I will go with these gentlemen and help with the coffee and let you see your daughter for a few minutes before I come and talk to her." With that Randy turned and led the way to the cafeteria with Barry and Steve close behind.

Chett looked at Cynthia and with a weak smile he turned and walked to the door of the waiting room. Taking a deep breath, he prayed for God's strength and pushed the door open. All three ladies jumped at the sound of the door and Chett watched as Sydney looked at him and slowly realized who he was. She jumped from the chair and dropped her blanket as she ran to his arms. Holding his daughter, tears came to his eyes at the sounds of her sobs and broke his heart.

Hugging her closer, he whispered in her ear, "It's okay, Syd, I'm here." It was then that he realized that she was wet and cold. "Sydney, you're wet. You must be freezing. Let's get that blanket wrapped around you." Turning his daughter around they headed to the chair where she had been sitting. Anita had picked up the blanket and wrapped it around Sydney's shoulders as she sat down. Cynthia slipped silently into the chair that Anita had left vacant and drew her daughter into her arms. There they both cried as held on to each other.

Chett turned to Maria and asked, "So how are you doing, my dear? Jesse said that you brought her to the hospital and were with her when she got the call. Who called her?"

"Grant."

"What? How could Grant call her?"

"I'm not sure, but she was talking to Grant and when she collapsed, I picked up the phone and there was a man named David on the other end. He told me what had happened and that I should get Sydney to the hospital because that was where they were taking them. I heard him talk to some man named Randy to tell him that there was one male adult and three children." Maria started to cry as she remembered what had happened earlier at the house and the tragic turn life had taken.

Chett walked over and sat next to Maria and drew her into a hug. Maria had always been like a daughter to him and he felt for her as she had to take charge and was just now letting it all sink in. "Maria, did you say Randy?"

"Yes, that was the name of the man that this David was talking to."

"Randy is here and I just talked to him before I came in here. He was at the accident and he rode in the ambulance with Grant and Brendan. He went for some coffee with Barry and he has agreed to come and talk to Sydney and tell her about the accident." Chett released Maria and realized that she was just as wet and cold as his daughter. "You two need some dry clothes."

"Yes you're right, I am starting to get uncomfortable in these wet clothes." Maria knew they both needed dry clothes but also knew that Sydney wouldn't leave the hospital until she knew that condition of her family, even then she would probably stay.

"I could go and get some dry clothes for you both." Anita had been sitting quietly in the opposite corner waiting for her husband to come back and wondering what she could do to be of some help. "That way you could both stay here and wait for news."

"I hate to ask you do that." Maria really wanted dry clothes but hated for someone to make a special trip to get them for her.

"Really, I would love to do this for you both. Just tell me what to get and where they are. You both would feel so much better with dry warm clothes." Anita rose and found a paper and pen in her purse to write the list down. After getting complete instructions from Maria and a few more from Sydney, Anita took their house keys and headed out to her car, telling them she would be back as soon as possible. As Anita left the waiting room and headed to the parking lot, from somewhere behind one of the doors to the emergency she heard a child scream. Anita's heart jumped and she immediately sent up a prayer for the crying child and the family of her friend somewhere within the walls of the hospital.

Sydney and Cynthia had dried their tears and were quietly talking as Maria and Chett watched the door open. Chett jumped up to help with the coffee and doughnuts that the guys had brought back. Helping to hand out the coffee, Steve noticed that Anita was not present.

"Maria, do you know where Anita went"? It wasn't that he was worried, he just wondered where she was and if she would need his help. She had been baking butterhorns when he stopped by the house to get her. She had immediately dropped everything and cancelled her Sunday School meeting that she had been baking for. Anita always loved to take something to the meetings. She said that everyone seemed more agreeable when there was food. She would often send some sort of baking to the church board meetings too, making all the board members extremely happy.

"Oh, she insisted that she go and get dry clothes for Sydney and I." Maria was thankful for the warm coffee, even if the taste left something to be desired. Steve smiled to himself as he thought how his wife could always find some way to help even in these sorts of situations. Her thoughtfulness made him proud of her and wishing that he had been that alert to the need before his eyes.

Sydney took her coffee but turned down the doughnut. She wasn't sure she wanted to drink the coffee either but holding the cup seemed to warm her hands. Looking around the room at all those who had gathered to await news on her family, she noticed a tall man in his late forties that she did not recognize. He stood in the corner looking extremely weary watching her and slowly sipping his own cup of coffee.

"Excuse me, but do I know you?" Sydney thought maybe she knew him from somewhere or maybe by asking him that, he would realize he was intruding and leave. The last thing she wanted was people just hanging around watching the poor widow.

"No ma'am, you don't know me. My name is Randy Moorehead." Randy didn't move and continued to sip his coffee.

"Well, Mr. Moorehead, is there a reason that you are here?" Sydney was starting to get a little annoyed with this man who wouldn't take the hint and leave.

"Sydney, Mr. Moorehead is a paramedic and he was at the accident." Chett looked over at Randy and gave him a nod, then continued, "Syd, he brought Grant and Brendan to the hospital and I asked him to come and tell you what happened."

Sydney's heart jumped when she heard Grant's name. This man knew about Grant.

"I'm sorry, Mr. Moorehead, you can tell me about my husband and the accident?"

"Yes ma'am."

"Please, have a seat and start from the beginning." Sydney sat up and hoped that this man would be able to tell her something to give her some hope for her family.

"If it's okay with you, I'd prefer to stand." Randy was

starting to feel weary of working his shift and feared that if he sat he would surely fall asleep.

"Yes, whatever you like, please just tell me about my husband." Sydney remembered Grant's last words to her, *"Syd, I love you." Oh Grant, I love you too! Please, please be alright.*

Randy proceeded to tell Sydney what he saw when he got to the accident scene. His friend David O'Rielly had been at the Gillman's truck on the driver's side attending to Mr. Gillman. After checking all the other passengers, they decided to take the oldest boy and Mr.Gillman first due to the seriousness of their injuries. David had stayed to take care of the other two children while he transported the father and son. Randy told her about the other driver and that their truck had been totaled.

"Mr. Moorehead, were they all still alive when they got to the hospital?" Sydney was sure that her heart stopped while she waited for his answer.

"Yes, ma'am, they were all alive when they arrived here." But were they still? Randy didn't know the answer to that one.

At that moment the door opened and Dr. Katherine Hamilton entered. A small woman with long blonde hair she was usually smiling when Sydney saw her at church. But today she carried a somber expression, looking like a doctor with bad news.

"Sydney Gillman, I'm Katherine Hamilton. You know my mother, Dorothy?"

"Yes, I know who you are. Are you here to tell me about my family?"

"Yes, I was the doctor on duty and saw them all when they came into the ER. Joan, the head emergency nurse came and told me you were her and that I should come and talk to you as soon as we knew something. Well, I have some news and we need to talk." Katherine walked over to the chair that Chett had vacated for her and she sat down. "Sydney, we will start with your daughter."

Sydney's heart raced and her breathing was starting to feel labored as she waited to hear the fate of her beloved family.

CHAPTER THIRTEEN

Dr. Katherine Hamilton sat next to Sydney and saw the fear in her eyes. Katherine knew this wasn't easy for Sydney and had taken the first available moment to give her an update in the hopes of alleviating some of the fear. Katherine had seen Sydney and her family at church when she was able to attend with her mother, Dorothy. Katherine had moved to Spring Hills five years ago just after her father had died, to be near her mother. The busy ER at one of Chicago's biggest hospitals no longer held the excitement it once had after her father's death. Needing a change and feeling like she wanted to have more time with her mother, Katherine had come home to stay, at least for now. Finding a job had been easy and she was now the chief ER doctor in a trauma room that was considerably more quiet than her previous workplace in Chicago. The quieter life had also given her the opportunity to get to know the God she loved more and focus on being the doctor that God wanted her to be. Shortly after her move she had shortened her name at the hospital from Dr. Hamilton to Dr. Kat, saying that it was a good conversation piece and it eased the stress of the hospital visit for patients when they heard that Dr. Kat was taking care of them. The kids had taken to the name and any that had visited the ER now pointed her out and said hi when they saw her away from the hospital.

At this moment the nickname Dr. Kat was not going to ease the fear she was seeing in Sydney's eyes and knew that this was truly the worst part of her job. Katherine looked into the fearful eyes and prayed for wisdom and strength as she shared the condition of this family with a woman that had become very dear to her mother's heart. *Lord, give me the words to comfort this dear woman and please comfort her during the next few hours and days. Thank you for having her friends and family close at this time. Thank you for being here and for holding us each in the palm of your hand. I love you, Lord, Amen.*

"Your daughter Sarah is. . ." Katherine had started but was quickly interrupted by Sydney.

"Sarah Rose, she wants to be called Sarah Rose." Sydney clung to the hope that Sarah Rose was okay and the white casket would not need to be purchased.

"Yes. Sarah Rose. I did have that written down." Katherine smiled to herself as she remembered the bloodied little blonde girl admonishing her that her name was Sarah Rose and not just Sarah.

"How is she, Dr. Hamilton? Please tell me how my baby is." The waiting was just about too much to bear and Sydney was sure that she could bear no more.

"Well, she looked worse than she was when first arriving in the ER. Sarah Rose has a couple of deep lacerations on her forehead and face. From what Randy told me, she must have hit the center console on impact but because of her seatbelt and her brave brother in the backseat who tried to hold her back, her injuries are minimal. Head wounds have a tendency to bleed more and that explains all the blood we saw when she arrived. She is being stitched up right now and I would like to keep her in the ER for about another hour or so just to watch her but I think after that, she will be okay to go home." Katherine watched as the news slowly sank in and was relieved to see some of the fear dissipate from Sydney's eyes.

"Dr. Hamilton, are you sure she can come home tonight? And will there be much scarring on her face?" Sydney couldn't believe she asked that last question. It's not like she was really worried about that, she was just so relieved that Sarah Rose was going to be okay. Now if only her boys and her dear husband had faired as well.

"Yes, I am sure that she can go home and the scarring should be minimal. Dr. Walcott is with her now. He's a plastic surgeon and was here at the hospital when Sarah Rose came in. I asked him to take care of her because he has a real gift and he agreed. Although your daughter was none too happy to have to be sitting still to be stitched up. She is very concerned about the welfare of her brothers and her daddy and wants to be with them. She can be very...shall we say...insistent? So we promised that she could see one of her brothers as soon as she was stitched and cleaned up a little. As soon as Dr. Walcott is finished, I will have Joan take you back to see her." Katherine knew that little Sarah Rose was a force to be reckoned with when she had placed her hands on her little hips and demanded that she see her daddy and brothers. It had taken all of their persuasive powers to get her to wait. Katherine had to hide her laugh as she stood there watching the scene unfold, knowing that she had once been just like that.

"Doctor, how are my boys and my husband?" Sydney was relieved to hear about Sarah Rose and was proud of her concern for her brothers and father, but there still lingered the fear for her boys and she needed to know how they were.

"Please just call me Katherine or Dr. Kat, whichever you prefer. Now the boy that came in with Sarah Rose was. . ." Again Sydney interrupted Katherine.

"Scott, that was my Scotty. I saw him from the parking lot when they brought him in. How is he?" Sydney remembered seeing all the blood and Scotty's matted, curly brown hair. The memory struck fear in her heart as she remembered how still and lifeless he had seemed. Sydney closed her eyes at the memory and waited for the news that would tear her world apart.

"Yes, Scott." Katherine paused as she watched Sydney close her eyes and seemed to brace herself for bad news. Katherine's heart jumped at the fear and apprehension that filled this woman knowing that whatever news she heard, she always expected the worst. Sydney mouthed the words, *"Oh, Scotty"* as Katherine continued.

"Well, Scott was in the back seat with Sarah Rose and as I said earlier had tried to hold her back when they hit. The force of the impact and his sister has broken his forearm. He is waiting to be X-rayed but I am sure that we will be able to set and cast his arm without much trouble. Scott also has some facial lacerations from hitting the back of the seat, but again, Dr. Walcott has agreed to take care of those so that there will be minimal scarring. Once we get the x -rays back and see what kind of fracture we are dealing with, we should be able to deal with his arm right away and then he should be able to go home. He will be in some pain and I will prescribe some mild pain medication for him. He will need to keep it elevated for a day or two so that there is a minimal amount of swelling. Otherwise, he is a very brave and strong young man."

"But, he was so still and looked lifeless when they brought him in, are you sure that he only has a broken arm?" Sydney couldn't believe that he was okay, it just did not register with what she had seen in the parking lot earlier.

"Yes, he only has a broken arm. He was in quite a bit of pain from the break when he arrived and was pretty pale. Moving at all was painful and so that's why looked so still.

We have given him some pain medication and cleaned him up a bit while he waits to be taken to x-ray. Once we get the x-rays and get his arm taken care of, then it shouldn't take Dr. Walcott too much time to stitch him up." Katherine could understand Sydney's concern, Scott had looked quite still and rather pale when he came into the ER and was very concerned about his father and older brother. Having ridden in the ambulance with his sister had calmed some of his fears about her safety and he was eager to see her and the rest of his family.

The door squeaked as it was opened and Nurse Joan Patterson entered carrying some nurse's scrubs and a couple of sweaters. Feeling like she had just walked in on a very serious conversation, she felt immediately uncomfortable.

"Uh, I just brought some dry clothes for the two ladies that were cold and wet. A couple of the nurses sent their sweaters and scrubs over, hoping to help." A stout nurse in her fifties, Joan Patterson was accustomed to dealing with all sorts of people in the ER as head triage nurse, but the grief and pain apparent in the young mother's eyes shook her and she had sprung into action trying to find some dry clothes and some sweaters for the two women. Watching Sydney sink to the floor in the lobby, screaming for her son, had pierced her heart and Joan made sure she let Dr. Kat know she was here and that she should talk to her as soon as possible. Joan was herself a grandmother and was thankful for all the family and friends that had come to be with Sydney. Joan took the items over to Maria and gave them to her. Turning, she looked at Dr. Kat and said, "Dr. Hamilton, Dr. Sinclair has asked that you come right away. He needs to talk to you about the CAT scan results." Turning to leave she spotted Randy and whispered to Him, "Randy, David is here looking for you, he's in the cafeteria."

"Thanks, Joan, I will go there right away. How was he when he came in?" Randy was concerned for his friend.

David was pretty shaken up and Randy knew that this accident was going to haunt his friend for quite a while.

"He was some upset when he got here. I sent him to the cafeteria and told him I would find you and send you there." With that Joan opened the door and left. Holding the door open, Pastor Steve had overheard the exchange with the nurse and Randy.

"Excuse me, Randy? I'm Pastor Steve. Would you like me to come with you to talk to your friend? I know the family quite well and may be of some help." Steve thought that he may be able to help in some way knowing that this fellow had witnessed the accident.

"Sure, that would be great, Pastor I may need to talk to you too. This accident has hit me pretty hard too." At that, Randy and Steve left the waiting room heading for the cafeteria.

Katherine knew that the news about the CAT scan was about Grant and although she was anxious to hear the news, she was torn about leaving Sydney with news about only two of her family members.

"Sydney, I really need to go talk to Dr. Sinclair. I'll be back as soon as I can to tell you about Brendan and Grant. We're still waiting on some test results and as soon as I get them, I'll come talk to you. Are you going to be okay?" Katherine didn't want to add to the fear she saw in Sydney's eyes but knew that she had to do her job and take care of this woman's family.

"Dr. Kat, was it?" Chett could see the protest coming from his daughter and knew that he needed to intervene so that Dr. Kat could get on with the treatment of his grandchildren and son in law.

"Yes, Dr. Kat is what I am called around here." Katherine turned to look at the man who was talking to her. He was in his late fifties and had a marked resemblance to Sydney in his graying, blonde, curly hair and green eyes.

"Dr. Kat, you go and take care of our family and we will be fine. Don't worry about us; just take special care of our loved ones. And thank you so much for coming and telling us about Sarah Rose and Scott. That helps us so much knowing that they'll be coming home tonight." Chett knew that he liked this young doctor and that his family was in good care with her.

Katherine stood and was thankful for the support that Sydney had. "I will take the best care of your family that I can and be back as soon as I have the test results. I can give you some firm facts on their conditions at that time." Katherine squeezed Sydney's shoulder and then turned and left the room heading to her meeting with Dr. Sinclair.

Sydney couldn't believe that she had just left without telling her about Grant and Brendan. Sydney turned to her father and said, "Why did you let her go? I need to know how Grant and Brendan are. Why did you do that?"

Chett moved to the seat that had been vacated by Katherine and put his arm around Sydney. "Sydney, she had to go and take care of them. The CAT scan results could have been about one of them. We know about the two little ones and we should be thankful to God that they were not hurt worse. Syd, we just need to keep praying for Brendan and Grant. They are in His hands and He will take care of them."

"God. Why would I pray to Him? He's the one who did this to my family. You pray if you want but please do not include me in those prayers to a God who doesn't seem to care." Sydney couldn't believe that this was happening and her anger rose towards the God who had done this to her. After all she had done to try to placate Him and now He was exacting His revenge on her for having a great life without Him. Well, a great life besides the fear, nightmares and the fact she thought that she was going crazy. But then again, it was probably His plan to drive her crazy any way.

"Syd, God loves you and He loves your family! He didn't do this to you." Chett was stunned by his daughter's accusations and didn't quite know how to respond. He knew that she had accepted God as a child and had lived what appeared to be a thriving Christian life, but this hatred she was venting took him aback.

"No, He does not love me, He wants revenge on me for my perfect life. He is trying to give me trials and persecutions, but I have had it and I will not follow a vengeful God anymore!" Sydney stood and looked around the room. Everyone here loved this so-called "good God" and the last thing she needed was for them to gang up on her at a time like this. Heading towards the door of the waiting room, Sydney hissed, "I am going to see if I can see my daughter. You are all free to stay here and pray all you want." And with that she was gone, leaving everyone in the room startled and unbelieving of what they had just witnessed

CHAPTER FOURTEEN

Sydney walked towards the nurse's station seething about what was said in the waiting room and about the doctor leaving when she did not know how her whole family was. Well, she was going to do something about that right now. The nurse that everyone had called Joan was sitting at the desk going over some papers. The audacity of her to just sit there when she should be doing something to help her family! Sydney approached the desk and her temper had her poised to give somebody a piece of her mind.

"Excuse me, but isn't it about time I was able to see my family?" It took everything Sydney had within her to not scream at the nurse and demand her rights. She felt like she was going to explode from all the strain and worry of the last couple of hours. She could hardly bear the thought of what happened to her family and then her dad had to go and bring up God. That was the last straw and she knew that she just couldn't sit there and listen to that while she wondered how her husband and son were.

Joan jumped, as she had been totally absorbed in getting the admitting forms for Mr. Gillman and his one son ready. Dr. Kat had stopped by on her way to the second floor where the CAT scan was to meet with Dr. Sinclair and told her to prepare the forms and to also get surgery authorization forms ready to be signed by Mrs. Gillman.

"Oh, Mrs. Gillman, you startled me. I'll go see if Dr. Walcott is finished with your daughter. I'm sure she will be very happy to see you." Joan jumped up and hurried down the hall to check on Sarah Rose, leaving Sydney standing there, angry and confused. *Why would God single her out and give her all this death? First Grandma Ruth, then both of her Forrester grandparents in a single accident and now her whole family in another accident. What did she ever do to incur such wrath from God? She had read about all the times He had leveled His wrath at the Israelites and the nations that had persecuted them and now she wondered why she was being targeted by His anger? No, she could never call Him a God of love and the last thing she would do was call Him Father.*

Just then Joan called her name and as she looked up, she saw the stout nurse hurrying down the hall towards her. "Mrs. Gillman, the doctor said that you can come in and see your daughter. Just follow me this way, my dear, and we will get you reunited with that precious little girl of yours."

Relief flooded Sydney as she thought about seeing her sweet little girl. Following Joan, Sydney had all she could do to not break out in a run to see Sarah Rose. The only thing holding her back was that she did not know what room she was in. As they walked down the hall and approached a door on the right, Sydney heard the sweetest words ever by the voice that made her heart sing.

"Now, Dr., will you let me see my brothers and my daddy? And where is my mother? She will be so worried when we don't show up with pizza for supper. I think that I am cleaned up enough to see my brothers, now show me where they are." Sarah Rose was very insistent about seeing the rest of her family and Sydney knew just how stubborn she could be. Sydney hurried past Joan towards the voice of her daughter, and as she stepped around the curtain, she stopped short as she looked at the swollen bandaged face of her daughter.

"Sarah Rose?"

"Mommy!"

With that exclamation, Sydney ran to her daughter and took her into her arms and held her close as she wept with relief that her precious little girl was going to be alright.

Back in the waiting room Maria stood holding the dry clothes that Joan had brought for her and Sydney. "Chett, Cynthia, I am sorry. I should have told you sooner about Sydney." Maria was overcome with a sense of weariness and was unsure about how to tell the family of her best friend that she had seen the fear and the change in Sydney but was unsure of how to help her or stop it. Many times she had tried to talk to Sydney but she had been shut down and now she wished that she had been more insistent with Sydney and not back down with the excuse that she didn't want to hurt their friendship. It was true what they said about hindsight always being 20/20.

"Well, we have time now. This is quite a change. Please sit, my dear, and tell us what has been going on with our daughter." Chett moved over one chair so that Barry could sit next to his wife who was going to sit next to Chett as she shared the change in Sydney. Barry reached over, taking the dry clothes and placing them on the table beside him. He took his wife's hand and gave it a gentle squeeze as she began.

"Well, it all started when you and Cynthia took Ruth to the hospital the last time and how Sydney had been so sure that Ruth was dead and we had prayed for her. I worried about Sydney even then because she seemed so unsure about God really being with her or even hearing her. When Ruth had died, I saw a change in Sydney that has always bothered me. Although she talked like a Christian and was involved in many church activities, I sensed there was a void in Sydney that wasn't being filled. When I asked about her daily devotions, Sydney just replied that things were okay and that she was just so busy doing things for God that she was sure He would forgive her lack of daily Bible reading. I tried to talk to her, but she just wouldn't listen and told me to not worry. If only I had worried more! After Sydney and Grant married, she had become involved in the church, undertaking many jobs and always keeping herself busy. Sydney would talk a little about God, but never in a personal way. I sensed that Sydney was looking for a feeling from God and was questioning how to get it. Then Hans and Esther were killed and again I saw the change in Sydney. About that time, Grant shared with me about the nightmares that Sydney was having. He was sure there was a connection to the recent deaths of her grandparents and the dreams, but Sydney would only say that they were falling dreams. Grant thought that maybe I could get her to open up about them since we have been friends for so long, but since the accident, every time I tried to talk to her about God, she refused to continue the conversation. Sydney continued to serve in the various church activities but refused to talk about God at all with Grant or me. About a year ago or so, the nightmares started up again. Grant would always phone me when she had one and it seemed that after every dream she would come to my house the next day. I tried to talk to her, but she always shut me down and now I am wishing that I had been more insistent. Chett, I am so sorry I have failed your daughter and my best friend and now she is turning away from the God who loves her more than she realizes." Maria broke down in tears and turned and buried her face into Barry's chest. Barry held her and let the tears flow because he knew the strain this had been on his wife. He was relieved that others now knew so that she would not have to carry this burden alone.

Chett was stunned by the reaction of his daughter when he had brought up God and now he was even more concerned. He hadn't realized how much Sydney had blamed God for the deaths in her family and now he also wished that he had been more attentive to her needs. Chett shook his head in disbelief and reached for the hand of his wife. Cynthia had silently started to weep as she heard about the change in her daughter. Looking up at Chett and then over to Maria who was crying in Barry's arms, Cynthia's voice broke as she said, "The best thing that we can do now is pray. Pray for the children and Grant and especially for Sydney. She is going to need God more now than ever before and we need to pray that she will realize how much He loves her."

Chett marveled at the strength of his wife and the deep faith she had especially in times of tragedy. Squeezing her hand, he reached over and grabbed Maria's hand and said, "Yes, the best thing we can do is pray. We need to ask the Lord to bring someone into Sydney's life that she will listen to and will be able to show her God without her blinders of fear. I'll start...."

The room quieted as Chett started to pray for his daughter and her family. Each person clung to the hands of those beside them and they each took a turn bringing their loved ones before the throne of grace. Each was pleading for wisdom for the doctors as they treated Brendan and Grant, thanking God for the minor wounds of Scotty and Sarah Rose and that they would be able to come home so soon. Then they each prayed for Sydney and that God would show His love for her in a way that she should understand and accept. When they finished praying, they all sat quietly, listening to the hustle and bustle of the emergency room outside of the waiting room door. Silently, they all waited for someone to walk through the door with news of their loved ones.

CHAPTER FIFTEEN

Sydney clung to Sarah Rose, not wanting to let her go, feeling like if she did then she would be gone forever. She just couldn't believe that her precious little girl was okay. As Sydney slowly released Sarah Rose, she looked again at the swollen face that was already starting to show signs of bruising.

"Sarah Rose, how are you feeling? I was so worried about you." Sydney couldn't say more for fear of breaking down into tears once more. The sight of her daughter brought such joy to her heart even though she still wondered at the fate of her oldest son and husband.

"Mommy, it was soooo scary. The big truck just came right at us and Daddy tried to turn but the truck just hit us. Scotty tried to hold me and I heard Brendan yell at Daddy to watch out. Mommy, the other truck was sooo big." Sarah Rose rattled on at a hundred miles an hour telling her mother about all that happened and the ride in the ambulance. She talked about Jack and how he had taken such good care of Scotty and how the doctor had been named "Dr. Kat." Sydney listened to her daughter and just gazed in wonder at how close she had come to losing her.

"Mommy, they won't let me see Daddy, Brendan or Scotty. I need to know how they are and they will not let me see them. Have you seen them, Mommy?" Sarah Rose could be so determined and Sydney smiled for the first time as she answered her daughter.

"No sweetie, I have not seen anyone except for you. Dr. Kat came to talk to me and told me all about you and Scotty but she was still waiting for some test results before she could tell me about Brendan and Daddy." Sydney's heart jumped as she thought about Grant and Brendan, hoping that they would be able to come home today as well, but deep inside, she knew that it would not happen that way.

"How is Scotty? Mommy, he was so brave—he tried to hold me and keep me from getting hurt." Sarah Rose started to tear up as she talked about her brother and Sydney knew that they both needed to see Scotty for their peace of mind. Sydney turned to the large male nurse who was cleaning up around the room they were in.

"Excuse me, I was wondering—do you know where my son Scott is? I would like to see him." Sydney sounded more in control then she felt.

"Your son was up in the x-ray room but I will see if he is back. Dr. Walcott was waiting to stitch up the boy's lacerations when he came back from x-ray. I will be right back." Jason Turner left the room and headed down the hall to check out where the boy named Scott was. Jason was a large man of thirty years who loved working in the ER, and when the family had come in, his heart went out to those who were waiting for news. Jason loved children and hoped one day to have a family of his own—that is, once he found a wife. He admired Dr. Kat and wanted to ask her out but he wasn't sure that she would go out with an ER nurse with whom she worked. Lost in his thoughts, Jason looked up just in time to see Dr. Kat coming off the elevator.

"Dr. Kat, " Jason yelled to get her attention and hurried

his pace to try and catch up to her.

"Oh Jason, how is Sarah Rose doing?" Katherine was worried about Grant Gillman and was wondering how she was going to tell Sydney, when she saw Jason.

"She is all cleaned and stitched and her mother is with her right now. They are waiting to see Scott so I was trying to find out where he was for them. How are the other boy and the father?" Jason had heard the details of the accident from Randy when he brought the first two in and was angered at the irresponsibility of some drivers.

Katherine shook her head and Jason knew that the news was not good. He had seen her look this way before and he admired the way she had compassion for the families and did her best for the patients, often going above and beyond to try and assure the best care. That was one of the reasons why he liked her and maybe one day he would be able to tell her.

"Jason, I am going to need to talk to Mrs. Gillman but I would like her to be with those of her family in the waiting room. I really do not want the children to hear what I have to tell her. They have been through enough today. Scott is on his way back from x-ray. I stopped in there and saw him. When he gets here, let them in to see him for a few minutes before I set and cast his arm and then we will let Dr. Walcott finish up. After that, take care of the daughter and let me know when Mrs. Gillman has gone back to the waiting room. I need to go talk to Joan about surgery consent forms. Thanks Jason." Katherine turned and walked to the head nurse's station and Jason turned and headed back to the room where Mrs. Gillman was.

As Jason entered the room he watched as Sydney slowly rocked her daughter in her arms while the little girl talked about her day. Jason knew that whatever the news about the rest of her family, he was glad that they had each other, for he could see the deep bond that they had. Hating to disturb them, he cleared his throat trying to get their attention.

"Mrs. Gillman, your son will be down right away from x-ray and the doctor said that you and your daughter could have a few minutes with him before they set his arm. If you will follow me I will take you to the room that he will be in and you can wait for him there."

Sydney looked up and saw the sympathy in this man's eyes and knew that he knew something about Grant and Brendan and he was feeling sorry for her. Sydney set Sarah Rose down on the bed and rose .

"You know something about my husband and son, don't you?"

"Mrs. Gillman, I don't know anything except that Dr. Kat is wanting to talk to you after you see your son." Turning and retrieving a wheelchair from behind the door, Jason continued, "Now let us go and see your brother, and because you have had a bump to the head and you are a patient here, you get to ride in this wheelchair, Miss Gillman."

Giggling, Sarah Rose let Jason move her to the wheelchair and she turned to her mother and said "Mommy, he called me Miss Gillman." Laughing again as Jason started out of the room, giving her what he called the special ER parade ride through the halls of the emergency room.

Following slowly behind, Sydney's heart was once again gripped with fear at the news that awaited her. *How would she go on without Grant and Brendan? Life would never be the same. Silently she yelled out at God "Why me? Haven't you done enough?"* Sydney was brought back to the present as Sarah Rose laughed wildly while Jason zigged and zagged her down the hall to the last door on the left and then swung into the room, which brought forth yet another round of giggles from her daughter. Just as they entered the room and Jason pulled the chair from the corner out for Sydney, a gurney was wheeled in carrying a very quiet boy with brown, curly hair.

"Scotty," Sarah Rose yelled and tried to jump out of the

wheelchair, but Jason was too quick for her and grabbed her shoulder, keeping her from moving too far. Turning to look him in the face, she said, "Please let go of me, I have to go and see my brother."

"Yes, I know, Miss Gillman, but you need to wait and I will lift you up on to the bed beside him when they have the bed in place."

Sydney stood rooted to the spot as she watched Scott. He looked so pale and his left arm was in a temporary cast elevated by a pillow. His face was swollen and there was a gauze bandage on his forehead. He looked like he was going to have a couple of black eyes, but he was alive. Sydney's heart jumped for joy when he looked at her and slowly tried to smile and then whispered, "Mom."

Rushing to his side as the attendants pulled the Gurney into place and put the brakes on, she leaned over the side rail and kissed his face, "Scotty. . . I'm here for you." The tears came as Sydney took in the battered appearance of her son. He was alive—hurt but alive.

Jason lowered the side rail on the right side of the bed away from the broken arm and placed Sarah Rose next to Scott on the bed.

"Scotty, are you okay?" Sarah Rose stared wide-eyed at her brother, not knowing what to say. She had desperately wanted to see him but this didn't look like her brother.

"Sure Squirt, just banged up a bit. Don't worry about me. How are you?" Scott was feeling a little groggy from the pain medication but was thankful for it because the pain had been just about more than he could bear before they got to the hospital.

"I was so scared, Scotty...." Sydney listened as Sarah Rose told Scott all about what had happened to her and about the ride down the hall. Sydney couldn't believe that two of her children were going to be okay. Coming home tonight even—that was what the doctor had said. The relief that she felt was short lived as she remembered what the nurse had told her and the look in his eyes. Tears ran down her face as she knew that somehow she must now find the strength to go back to the waiting room and hear about the rest of her family. Feeling like the burden was too much for her, Sydney started to feel her knees become weak and grabbed for the stability of the rail on the bed. Jason had been watching Sydney and rushed to her side, grabbing her around the waist helping her to a chair in the next room that was vacant.

"Just sit here for a few minutes I am sure that your daughter will have quite a few stories for your son to keep him occupied for quite awhile. Mrs. Gillman, take your time, I will close the door and give you a few minutes to cry by yourself without anyone around. Here is a box of Kleenex. I will be right outside if you need something." Jason turned to leave the room and quietly closed the door.

Sydney couldn't believe that he would suggest that she cry. All she had done was cry from the moment she had heard the news. No, she had spent the last couple of hours trying not to cry with all her friends and family around. The tears started and soon Sydney let the full force of her tears flow, her anger at God, the fear of what the next news would be, the relief over Scott and Sarah Rose, and the unfairness of what had happened. Twenty minutes and half a box of Kleenex later, Sydney emerged from the room. Looking at Jason, she said, "I want to talk to Scott and Sarah Rose and then you can let the doctor know that I will be in the waiting room." Sydney headed to the bed where her children were talking and she turned and whispered to Jason, "Thank you, I guess I did need to cry."

Jason watched as Sydney walked up to the bed where her children were and talked to them. Hugging them both, she promised to be back as soon as she could but right now she had to go and find out how Brendan and Daddy were. After kissing them both she quietly left the room, heading back to the waiting room with what Jason thought looked like the burden of the world on her shoulders. Jason watched as the two children interacted while another nurse got everything ready to set and cast Scott's arm and stitch up his forehead.

"Jen, I am going to let Dr. Kat know that you are just about ready and that Mrs. Gillman is in the waiting room. I will be right back to take Miss Gillman to find some really special doughnuts." Seeing Sarah Rose and Scott laugh at his calling her Miss Gillman, Jason turned and went on his way to find Dr. Kat and let her know that the family was waiting for the news that she had for them.

CHAPTER SIXTEEN

The quietness of the waiting room was broken as the door squeaked, announcing the arrival of another person. Every occupant of the room looked to the door to see if the bearer brought news of their beloved family and friends who were somewhere within the walls of the hospital. Cynthia stood and quietly walked to the door and hugged her daughter. Pulling away slowly, she took Sydney by the hand and led her back to the chairs that lined the wall of the waiting room.

Sitting her between Chett and herself, Cynthia asked, "Syd, were you able to see the children?"

Feeling like the world was about to collapse on her, Sydney looked around the room at her parents and dear friends. She was struck at the quietness and the apparent peace that prevailed in the midst of tragedy. How could they have such a sense of peace when she felt like her whole world was going to come crashing down at any moment? Did they not know that grim news awaited them? Funerals were going to have to be planned and they seemed like everything was going to be okay. She wasn't sure whether she should be mad or just confused by all this.

"Yes, I saw Sarah Rose and Scotty. They both seem well considering all they have been through. They will both be released tonight." Sydney saw the relief and joy in the eyes of her parents but there was something else there that she couldn't identify. Why were they looking at her like that? It was something that she just couldn't put her finger on. What was it? As she tried to figure it out the door again announced someone else entering the room. As Sydney looked to the entrance she wondered why they hadn't fixed that door. It was getting to be rather annoying.

Peeking around the door into the waiting room was Hillary Gillman, Grant's baby sister. Seeing that she had the right room she turned and yelled behind her, "Hey, Kirby I found them. They're all in here." Turning back, she entered the room, holding the door open waiting for Kirby Hudson to catch up and enter the room also. As Kirby entered she quickly scanned the room and then rushed to her sister's side and took her into a long and sympathetic hug.

"Oh, Syd, this is just so awful. I just can't believe this. Have you heard anything or seen any of them?" Kirby was taller than Sydney and was quite thin. Built more like her father, Kirby looked more like her mother with her straight blonde hair and blue eyes. Sydney had always been jealous of Kirby's straight perfect hair while she struggled to tame curls that had a mind of their own. Sydney also admired her sister's outgoing personality and ability to ease everyone around her in any circumstance. Sydney released Kirby and sat back and looked into her blue eyes that were puffy and red from crying.

"You are right. This is awful and I can hardly believe this is happening. Yes, I was able to see Sarah Rose and Scotty." Sydney paused for she felt like she was not able to go on. The weariness and burden of it all was weighing her down. Looking up she again saw Hillary.

"Hello Hillary, have you talked to your parents? I am so sorry about Grant. We haven't heard anything about him or

Brendan yet but I was told that the doctor would be in soon to tell me about them." Now Sydney felt the fear and the dread of news that she knew was not going to be good. She did not have the strength to hold herself together, let alone help the sister of her husband when they found out.

"Syd, I talked to my parents just before I came to the hospital. They will arrive at ten o'clock tonight. I have to go to the airport to pick them up. They left me with strict instructions to phone them as soon as I had heard anything. So fill us in on the children while we wait." Hillary looked a lot like Grant, having dark brown hair and the same blue eyes that had transfixed Sydney when she had first met him. Sydney knew that Hillary would be hit hard by this accident because she had spent many hours babysitting the children and lived just a few blocks away while she finished her last year of college. She had become very close to Grant and had spent many hours at their place. Sydney sat back in her chair and took a long deep breathe and tried to get a hold of herself in order to share what had transpired over the last few hours. With great difficulty she related the story of the accident that Randy had shared with her, all the while thinking how surreal this whole thing seemed to her.

Next she told them of seeing her two youngest children and of their injuries to which both Kirby and Hillary replied "Thank you, Jesus, for their safety. "

Sydney was a little annoyed that they were thanking the God who had put her family in jeopardy in the first place. But not having the energy or the heart to say anything she just let it go like she hadn't heard it and continued on telling them that they were now waiting for news on Grant and Brendan.

Hillary rose and said, "I am going to go and phone Mom and Dad and let them know these latest details. I know that it will set them at ease to at least know what happened and that Sarah Rose and Scott are okay. I will be back shortly." With that Hillary left the room in search of a pay phone.

Kirby sat next to her sister, taken back by the fear and despair that filled her eyes. Kirby was glad that she had come to be with Sydney but was unsure what to do about the doubt that she had seen when she thanked the Lord for the children's safety. Surely the sister that she had idolized and strove to be like hadn't turned her back on God. That was almost too much for Kirby to bear.

Maria saw the concern in Kirby's face, "So did you come alone or is Brant with you?" she asked.

Kirby was jolted back to reality by the question and looked over at Maria, "No, after I phoned him he came right home and is taking care of the children. He was going to try and find a babysitter and come in. I was going to wait but he said that it was more important that I be here as soon as possible. We were just in shock when we heard. I still can't believe that this is happening." Turning to her mom she said, "Boy, am I glad that you guys came a day early."

"Yes we are thankful that we did also." Cynthia held tightly to her husband's hand and even though she felt concern for her grandson and son-in-law her heart was breaking over the change in Sydney. "I think that we were supposed to be here. I know that Sydney will need our help now. I think that your father and I will stay at Syd's tonight and take the children home for her. I am sure that she will want to remain at the hospital with Grant and Brendan until she knows how they are."

Sydney looked at her parents and wondered if they really believed that it was "God's doing" that they came a day early and were here for the accident that God had caused. Surely they realized that her family wouldn't be in this hospital if God had minded His own business and left her alone.

"You are right, Mom, I don't want to leave the hospital. I know that Sarah Rose would love for you to stay at our place. I think that if they stay at home they will feel more secure after what happened than if they stay somewhere else." Sydney shifted in her chair as she again thought about the possibility that her parents were here for a reason. Trying to put that thought out of her mind she continued, "Do you still have your key for our house? I am not sure where my keys are." Sydney felt for her keys in her pockets but was unsure where she had left them.

"You gave your keys to Anita. Remember, she was going to get us some dry clothes." Maria sat holding the clothes that Nurse Joan had brought for them. Maria had put on one of the sweaters but hadn't taken the time to go and put on any of the rest. "I have these clothes that the nurse brought. Would you like to go and change with me? It would probably make us a little more comfortable while we wait."

Realizing just how uncomfortable she was in the clothes that were wet and were now drying, Sydney knew that it was probably a good idea to change. But she just didn't want to leave the waiting room in case the doctor came with news.

"I know that I would feel a little better, but I just want to wait until the doctor comes before I go anywhere."

As she was talking the door to the waiting room again announced the arrival of someone. Looking towards the door, Sydney saw that Anita had returned carrying two small carry-on bags, one that she recognized as being Grant's. Anita looked around the room, noting the arrival of Kirby and the absence of Steve.

"Well, I have some dry clothes for you two. Are we still waiting for news or have we heard something?" Anita moved across the room to give Sydney her bag and keys and then gave Maria her bag and keys.

"We have heard about Sarah Rose and Scott but we are still waiting for news on Brendan and Grant." Maria took the bag and was deeply thankful for this act of kindness from Anita. Warm clothes would be great but the fact that they were her own made it wonderful.

Sensing the need to stay and wait, Anita replied, "How

about if we all leave the waiting room and I will guard the door so that you two can change. If the doctor comes while you are changing I can warn you to get decent quickly. That way, we won't have to go looking for you."

"What a great idea and thank you for going and getting those things for the girls, Anita." Cynthia rose and pulled her husband up beside her. "We will be just outside while you girls change. With all of us out there no one will disturb you as you change. Come on, Kirby, let's go and find Hillary and see if she was able to reach her parents. Barry, come and let's get some more coffee."

As they all left the room it became eerily quiet and Sydney and Maria were left sitting there holding their bags.

"Well, we had better get changed." Maria said but neither one moved.

"Maria, can you believed this is happening?" Sydney was still grappling with the events of the last few hours and desperately wished that she was dreaming.

"No. I can't believe this. But Syd, no matter what happens, I will be here for you and we will get through this together. God loves you and He loves your family." Maria had been silent long enough and she was now more concerned about her friend's future than about how she was going to react.

"Maria, I doubt that God loves me and what He did to my family shows me that He doesn't care about them either." Sydney sprung into action at the comment about God and started to change into the clothes Anita had brought her. Taking the clothes out of the bag, Sydney noticed that Anita had brought the navy sweatshirt that Grant had bought for her last Christmas. It was her favorite shirt and she wore it a lot. Slipping the shirt over her head she felt closer to Grant and her heart sank, as she thought about the fact that she may never see him alive again.

"Syd, God did not cause this accident. He loves you and you need to realize just how much He does love you." Maria had decided that although she didn't have all the answers about why the accident had happened, she was not going to let Sydney blame God and not confront it. Too long she had avoided it and now she regretted not helping her friend sooner.

"Maria, just leave it alone, I really don't have the energy to talk about this right now." Sydney turned her back to Maria hoping that she would take the hint and leave God out of the conversation. Sydney wondered why Maria would all of a sudden be so persistent. Surely she knew that Sydney didn't talk about God and wanted nothing to do with a God who was vengeful?

"Syd, for years I have watched you turn your back on God and blame Him for everything. I tried to talk to you about the dreams you had, but you refused. Grant was concerned and so am I. We love you Syd and I will no longer let you get by without talking about it." Maria felt new confidence as she talked and a sudden need to let her friend know just how much God loved her.

"I don't want to talk about it and Grant had no business telling you about my dreams. Besides, they were just falling dreams and there is nothing to worry about." Sydney wasn't sure she liked this change in Maria and definitely did not want to talk about the dreams with her. Why was she doing this now? Couldn't she see that everything she ever feared was coming true? Quickly pulling on her jeans she turned to Maria and asked, "Are you ready? Can I go and get the others?"

"Yes, I am ready but we will talk about this and Syd, I am praying for you and your family." Maria wished that they could talk more but also knew that the best thing she could do right now was pray for her friend. So for now she would let it go, but as soon as she could she was going to talk to Sydney and make sure that her best friend knew more about the God that Maria loved and could not live without.

CHAPTER SEVENTEEN

Sydney opened the door and just about ran into Anita who was standing there talking to Dr. Kat. Seeing the doctor, Sydney's heart jumped as she realized that she was probably there to let her know about Grant and Brendan. Sydney wasn't sure that she was going to be able to handle the bad news now. Why had Maria brought up God now? Couldn't she have left well enough alone? Sydney was so upset and confused that she was sure that the bad news that the doctor had would be the end of her.

"Dr. Kat, have you been waiting long?" Sydney's heart raced as she thought once again about the fate of her family in the news that the doctor had for her.

"No, actually I just got here and Anita was telling me that you were changing out of your wet clothes. I am glad that you were able to get some dry clothes. Now I won't have to worry that you might get sick." Katherine saw the fear in Sydney's eyes and was again struck by the hopelessness she saw there.

"Come in please, we were done changing. How are my husband and son?" Sydney held the door for Katherine and waited to sit until her parents, Kirby, Barry, Anita, and

Hillary had entered and found seats.

"Well, we have finished our tests, and things are as we first expected." Katherine paused because she knew that the news that she had wasn't going to be easy for the family. "Let's start with your son, Brendan." Again she paused as she looked around the room at those who were present. It was good to see Anita here also. She had seen and talked to Pastor Steve as he was on the way to the cafeteria with Randy. Katherine only hoped that Sydney would let her loved ones help her through this time.

"Brendan was sitting in the front seat and had his seatbelt on, thankfully. When he arrived at the hospital he was in respiratory distress and we had to intubate him. The problem persisted which indicated a possible tension pneumothorax, requiring that we place a needle into his chest to decompress it and then place a chest tube in. He has improved and will probably be able to have the chest tube out in a couple of days." Katherine again paused so that Sydney could get a handle on what had been said before she continued.

"Dr. Kat, will he be okay? What does the chest tube mean?" Sydney was trying to understand what was happening but was having a difficult time.

"Brendan will live, although he will not be released from the hospital right away. Brendan also has two broken ankles that will need surgery. I have Dr. Prescott checking the x-rays and he has said that he will take care of the ankles for Brendan. Dr. Prescott is a very good orthopedic surgeon and will take the best care of Brendan. As far as the chest tube, Brendan received quite a blow to the chest and there was fluid build up in his chest that was hindering his breathing. We have put the chest tube in to alleviate the pressure on his lungs and were pleased that there was no blood, which would have been cause for worry. Right now he seems to be doing okay and we have him sedated because of the intubation." Katherine watched as the realization that

Brendan was going to be okay washed over Sydney.

"Will Brendan be able to play baseball?" Sydney knew that Brendan lived for baseball and worried that he might take it hard if these ankle injuries kept him from playing. Sydney was feeling some relief that Brendan was going to be okay, eventually. Now if only Grant was okay.

"Brendan will not be playing this year, but if everything heals well and he is diligent with his physiotherapy, then he should be back playing next year. I understand that he loves baseball and was pitching for the high school team." Katherine knew that missing this year would probably be hard for Brendan but figured that he would work really hard in order to not miss next year as well.

"Yes, he was the pitcher. How did you know?" Sydney was curious as to how she would know since he wasn't able to talk and let her know that information.

"Oh, you can attribute my wealth of information to your daughter. While we were examining her she told us about everyone in her family." Katherine smiled as she remembered how hard it was to examine this little spitfire who chattered the whole time. She was thankful that Jason had been there and had been able to keep Sarah Rose entertained while they finished with the exam. Katherine admired Jason's dedication to his work and the gift he had with children. Children seemed to love Jason and Katherine was always thankful when he was there to help.

"Oh." Sydney knew that her daughter loved to talk and wondered what she had said about her mother. "How is my husband Grant?" Sydney had a feeling that the news about Grant would be more serious. She just hoped that she could see him soon and that he was still alive. Looking around the room at those who were there with her, she silently wished that there was a loving God who would answer her prayers and help Grant to be okay and would be coming home with her and their three children. But she knew there was only a vengeful and hateful God who had put her family in danger.

"I am afraid that he took most of the impact from the accident. His injuries are more serious." Katherine paused and watched as Maria moved to Sydney's side and grabbed her hand. Kneeling beside Sydney, Maria closed her eyes and silently prayed that God would comfort and bring peace to Sydney. Cynthia, who was sitting beside Sydney, reached for her other hand while Chett shifted in his chair. Everyone in the room braced themselves for the news in their own way as silence prevailed.

"Grant lost consciousness at the scene of the accident and has suffered a broken femur. We have placed his leg in traction to stabilize it until he can undergo surgery to repair the fracture. We will probably have to do intramedullary nailing but he will be fine with the traction stabilizing the leg for a day or two." Katherine had been quite concerned about the fracture but the immediate problem was why Grant Gillman was unconscious.

"Why can't you operate on his leg now if he needs the surgery? Why wait for a couple of days?" Sydney wasn't sure if she should be more worried in the fact that they were waiting or if she could finally believe that her entire family was going to be coming home.

"Well, the reason that we are waiting for a couple of days is because we are more concerned about Grant's head trauma than his fracture. Grant took quite a blow to his head and that has us quite concerned. The fact that he lost consciousness and has not regained consciousness is the reason that we sent him upstairs for a CAT scan." Katherine paused as she watched the fear replace the hope that had momentarily twinkled in Sydney's eyes.

"What are you saying? Is Grant dead?" Sydney felt the panic start to rise and she squeezed Maria's and Cynthia's hands, hoping that they would keep the panic from consuming her.

"No, he is alive but he has some accumulation of blood in his brain that is causing some pressure and we need to relieve that pressure as soon as possible. Dr. Sinclair is the staff neurosurgeon and I have consulted him and he is preparing for surgery now. Sydney, I will let you in to see Grant for just a few minutes before we take him in to surgery. He won't be conscious." Katherine was concerned that Sydney at least be able to see him in case the surgery took a turn for the worse. She hoped that it would bring some peace of mind if she was able to see that he was alive.

"Is there a chance that he won't make it out of surgery? Will there be brain damage? Will he hear me if I talk to him?" *Sydney wasn't sure how to feel. Her husband could still die, or worse yet, be a vegetable and never know who she is or be there for them again. She just wanted to scream at God and tell Him to leave her alone and that it wasn't fair. Grant had lived a great Christian life and loved God more then she did why was God doing this to him? Why?*

"Sydney, there is always a chance when someone goes into surgery. Dr. Sinclair is very good. We won't know if there is any permanent damage until he regains consciousness and we can assess him. Yes, I do believe that he will be able to hear you. I am going to get everything in order for the surgeries. Joan will come and get you and get you to sign some consent forms. After we have Grant ready for surgery, we will come and get you so you can have a few moments with him. Brendan will be going to surgery soon also and I will get you in to see him. Sydney, we will do everything that we can for them, I promise." Katherine stood and reached over and squeezed Sydney's shoulder. Turning, she walked to the door and paused when she heard Chett speak.

"Thank you, Dr. Kat, we really appreciate all that you have done already. We will be praying for you and the other doctors as you take care of Grant and Brendan."

"I will be back a soon as I can." With that Katherine left

the room and hurried down the hall to see to the Gillman family.

As the door closed the quietness surrounded the occupants of the room as they all tried to grasp the seriousness of the news that they had just heard. The silence was broken by strangled sobs as Hillary started to cry.

"How do I phone my parents and tell them this? I just can't do it, I just can't" Hillary dissolved into tears as Barry took her into his arms and held her like one of his own heart-broken daughters.

CHAPTER EIGHTEEN

The waiting room was silent. Maria sat next to Sydney holding her hand; Barry sat between Maria and Hillary with his eyes closed. Barry was known to fall asleep just about anywhere but tonight he was praying for his best friend and family. He closed his eyes so no one would distract him and so he could concentrate.

Hillary sat with her hands folded, wondering what she was going to tell her parents while she constantly watched the clock. It was nearly eight-thirty and soon she would have to leave for the airport to pick up her parents. She hoped that her parents had phoned her other brothers, Ryan and Don. When Hillary had gotten the news from her parents she had rushed out the door to the hospital, not even thinking to ask if Ryan and Don needed to be phoned. She knew that she did not have the strength to tell them either.

Chett and Cynthia also sat watching the clock, quietly holding hands. Chett had tried to phone their son Chad and let him know what had happened but had only gotten the answering machine. He had left a message to phone them at Kirby's as soon as he got home. Chett had then tried to get a hold of Brandy, Chad's fiancé but there again had only gotten the answering machine. Again, Chett left a message for her to get a hold of them at the hospital. Secretly he had hoped that she was working tonight in the ER and that she already knew. The quietness was broken by the ever annoying squeak of the door. Sydney jumped, hoping that it wasn't time to say good-bye to her husband yet. Before she saw the person entering the waiting room, she knew who it was.

Bursting into the room at a pace few could keep up with and talking at about one hundred miles an hour was Brandy. Pausing when she entered the room, she realized that she had been talking to herself out loud and that everyone was watching her.

"Oh Sydney, I just heard. I had been working the maternity ward this week filling in for a friend of mine and when my shift ended, I ran in to Joan and she told me what had happened. I just can't believe this. It is so awful! How are the children doing? Joan said that Sarah Rose and Scott are going home tonight but that Brendan and Grant were more serious." Stopping for a breath, she continued before anyone had a chance to answer her question. "Does Chad know? Probably not, he hasn't been home until late every evening this week because of his studying. His finals are finished next week and then he will be able to come home. Have you been able to see the children? I could see what I could do if you want? Have you heard about Grant and Brendan? I should go and see what I can find out." Everyone in the family who knew Brandy knew that when she got flustered that she had a tendency to just keep rattling on about nothing until someone was able to stop her. Cynthia got up and walked over to Brandy and put her arm around her. At that gesture, Brandy quieted.

"It's okay, we know what results they have about Grant and Brendan and Sydney was able to see the younger children. Come sit down and wait with us. Chett was going to go and try to call Chad again later. We left a message for him to call us at Kirby's but we never said why." Guiding her to the chair next to hers, they sat down and once again quiet descended upon the room.

Sydney shifted in her chair and wished that something would happen to distract her from the thoughts that kept plaguing her. *Could her parents be here for a reason? For some reason they think that God brought them here a day earlier to be with her. Did God really love her? Love her enough to arrange for her parents to be here for her? No, He was vengeful and it was His fault that this happened. He could have stopped it if He had wanted to. That just proved to her that He did not want to. But then again the words that Maria had been so forceful to say haunted her mind. "God loves you and your family." If God loved her family then why would He do this to them? Why had He taken her grandparents and Grandma Ruth? Surely if He loved them then He would have saved them? No, it all happened because she couldn't feel God and God was angry that she didn't have enough faith. God was punishing her, yet the thought of a God that loved her was a thought that would give her peace, if only it were true. How could this happen if He really loved her?* Sydney couldn't find a comfortable position in her chair and felt even more uncomfortable than when she had been wearing the wet clothes. *She had to go somewhere and think. Get her thoughts straight. Things were becoming blurry and she wasn't so sure what she believed any more. Why did everyone have to confuse her right now when she needed to keep her thoughts on her children and husband? Why couldn't they keep their thoughts about God to themselves? Now they have her fantasizing about a God who loves her instead of accepting the reality of the vengeful and hateful God who had so deeply hurt her family.* Standing to her feet, Sydney looked at everyone in the room and knew that she needed to go somewhere else and think. *Somewhere where she could get her perspective and clear her head, but where?*

Announcing another visitor to the waiting room, the door squeaked to a halt as Dr. Kat stood in the doorway holding the door wide open.

"Sydney, we are ready for you to see Brendan. We are still getting Grant ready but by the time you are done seeing your son he will be ready. Follow me." Turning and holding the door for Sydney, she followed her out the door. "Brendan is upstairs waiting to go into surgery. He has been sedated and looks little rough but I know that he will hear you and your presence and comfort will help him before he goes into the operating room." Katherine pushed the third floor button as they stepped into the elevator and the doors slid closed. All was quiet except for the sound of the elevator as it moved upwards to the surgery floor. Sydney leaned against the wall looking like she was too weary to stand on her own. Katherine was worried that the shock of seeing her husband and son may be too much for her right now.

"I know that you want to see them but you don't have to. They look pretty rough and you probably won't recognize them right away. It's okay if you are not up to it right now." Katherine knew that seeing family members after accidents was hard on loved ones but she also knew that if they could do it that it benefited the patients. Knowing that they were not alone always helped.

"I want to see them. I know that they will not look the same but I have to let them know that I am here. I need to see them in case they . . . they…they don't. . . " Sydney just couldn't bring herself to say out loud what she was thinking.

"Sydney, Brendan is going to be okay and we feel that we are getting to Grant in good time and that is the most important thing." Just then the doors opened to the third floor and the noise and bustle broke the quiet of the elevator. Stepping out of the elevator, Katherine held the door for Sydney and then they proceeded down the hall to pre-op. As they entered the room the smell of antiseptic overwhelmed the senses and Sydney watched as nurses did their checks on the only patient in the room. Taking a closer look, Sydney recognized a pale and bruised Brendan. He was covered with a blanket from the chin down and she was relieved that she could not see the chest tube and the broken ankles. Just seeing his deathly looking face was enough to scare her. Rushing to his side she leaned over the rail and placed her hand on his face. Gently touching his face and hair, she whispered in his ear.

"Brendan, Mom is here." Sydney struggled with the tears but she tried to keep her voice as strong as possible for her son. "Brendan, everything is going to be alright. I will be right here and will not leave you. Please be okay, Brendan, you are my first boy and I love you. Please be strong and come home with me."

Not being able to say more, she kissed his forehead and continued to stroke his hair. How could this have happened to her baby? Tears streamed down her face and dropped to the sheet next to Brendan's head.

"Brendan, Mom loves you and I know that Dad loves you too. Grandma and Grandpa Forrester are here and so are Aunt Kirby and Hillary. They are all waiting to see you. Take care, my boy, and be strong. Everything is going to be okay." Again the sobs threatened to keep her from talking and she just stood there looking at her son. He was so strong and looked like his father. He was so young yet and has hardly begun to live and now he will have to go through physiotherapy and probably struggle with ankle problems all his life. *This just is not fair, how could this have happened?*

"Sydney, Dr. Prescott is ready for Brendan." Katherine had left Sydney with Brendan and had cleared the room so that she could be alone. "They have brought Grant up and he is in the next room. I will take you over there right now and you should be able to spend some time with him before they are ready." Katherine led the way as Sydney followed her across the hall and into the room where Grant was hooked up to all kinds of machines.

Sydney gasped as she looked at Grant, his leg attached to some kind of traction device on the end of his bed and the left side of his head shaved. The left side of his face was bruised and he was extremely pale. If it weren't for the machines beeping she would have thought that he was dead. Rooted to that spot, she felt unable to move her feet and felt like everything around her was growing dark. Sydney struggled for breath as Katherine grabbed her around the waist and lowered her into the chair by the bed.

"Sydney, take some deep breathes. It's okay. Now breathe." Katherine had been concerned about this when she had brought Sydney up here, but when she had not passed out with Brendan, she thought it was going to be okay.

Sydney closed her eyes and tried to take in some deep breaths. Slowly the darkness faded away and she felt ready to talk to Grant, relieved that she had not passed out and missed being able to spend maybe her last time with him. Opening her eyes, she looked into the concerned eyes of Katherine and whispered, "I'm ready."

"Okay, if you are sure? I will move this chair up beside his head so that you can sit while you talk to him. Okay?"

"That would be fine." Sydney stood and waited for Katherine to move the chair before she once again took her seat.

"I will leave you alone. You probably have about twenty minutes before they come and take him into surgery. I will come and get you when it's time." Quietly she slipped from the room and left the husband and wife alone.

Taking Grant's hand, Sydney was struck by how cold it was. Placing it in-between her two hands she started to rub his hand to get it warm. As she rubbed his hand she felt his wedding ring. Looking down at the wide white gold band, she remembered the day that she had slid it on to his finger and vowed to love, honor and cherish until death.

"Oh, Grant it's too soon. We have hardly had any time together. Please don't leave me. I won't be able to go on with out you. I love you more then life itself. Oh Grant. . ." Again the tears came and she leaned her head against his arm and gave way to the flood of tears.

CHAPTER NINETEEN

Sydney's tears had slowly subsided and she had eased herself up onto the bed beside Grant. There was little room and she struggled to stay on the bed but being near him in this way comforted her. She had placed his hand on his chest and was still rubbing it with her one hand as she clung to the bed with her other. *Why had this happened? Did God really hate her that much that He would take away her only reason for living? Why?* Nothing was clear anymore and things were more confused then ever.

In a quiet whisper that she herself could barely hear her soul cried out, *"God, why are you doing this to me? I have tried to live a life that I thought you wanted. Is it because I can't feel you? Is it because I don't have enough faith? Why? I just don't understand. I don't know what you want. But please don't take Grant away from me. Please, please don't take him away."* As she continued to rub his hand she slid her hand under his and her heart jumped. Grant had ever so slightly given her hand a gentle squeeze.

"Grant, I love you. Please be strong and stay with me. Don't leave me, please, honey don't leave me." Sydney started to cry once again at the hope that Grant would be okay and that maybe this was all just a dream. Just then Katherine entered the room.

"Sydney, they are ready for Grant now. I'll walk with you back down to the waiting room." Katherine waited and watched as Sydney slid from the bed and kissed Grant good-bye. Turning slowly, Sydney followed Katherine from the room as nurses and orderlies entered the room to set about moving Grant to the operating room.

"Is there somewhere else that I could go to wait for them to get out of surgery?" Sydney knew that she just could not bear waiting in the room with everyone else right now. Her mind was in a state of confusion and she just needed to be alone.

"Well, there are only two places that would not have any other people right now, the waiting room outside of the ICU or the chapel." Katherine had seen what she thought was Sydney praying for her husband and thought that maybe she wanted to be alone to pray.

Thinking to herself, Sydney wasn't sure that the chapel was the best place for her in her present state of mind but then again sitting outside of the ICU wasn't where she wanted to be either. "I guess the chapel will have to do. Is it near by?"

"Yes, it is on the second floor and we will be able to find you quickly when they are out. I will take you there." Katherine pushed the button for the elevator and was happy that they did not have to wait long. Katherine's shift had been over about an hour ago and now that everyone was being taken care of she was free to go home. Feeling weary, Katherine knew that the events of today were going to be with her for quite sometime. Maybe some time in the quiet chapel would do her good before she went home.

When the elevator arrived to the second floor, Katherine led the way down the hall to the chapel. Entering the chapel, Katherine was immediately comforted by the quiet surroundings. Along the walls, replica stained windows were lit from behind by lights, giving the room the feel of outside windows. Six oak pews sat in rows and each row boasted its own Bible for those who came to be comforted by its words. A crucifix was mounted on the wall behind a small oak table that displayed a larger Bible that was always opened. Katherine wasn't sure who took care of the chapel but everyday the bible was turned to a different passage, and whenever she was on this floor, she would stop in just to read the daily selection. Walking to the front she read the selected passage and then returned to the last pew where she sat down and bowed her head.

Sydney had watched Katherine and wondered why she wasn't leaving. Realizing that she would not be leaving soon, Sydney resigned herself to company and hoped that no questions would be asked. Sliding onto the pew second from the front on the opposite side as Katherine, Sydney sat there wondering why she was even here. God had abandoned her and here she was in the place where if she wanted to talk to Him, this would be the most logical place.

Why was she here? She did not want to talk to God. He was the one who had caused all this and there was no way that she wanted to talk to Him. Yet, she wanted to know why He was doing this to her. But where would she begin, for it had been a very long time since she had talked to Him and even then He never answered. Why would she expect an answer now, yet her heart was weighing her down and she felt the need to at least ask why? Why had this happened? Why did God not love her like He did everyone else? Why could she not feel Him? Why had He turned on her? Why Grant? Why her children? Why the dreams? Why her grandparents? God, why is this all happening to me? Why do you hate me? Sydney's heart was breaking and she had no answer to her questions. At that moment everything in her broke forth with a loud cry towards heaven that filled the chapel and echoed off the walls, "Why God, why?"

Katherine was jolted from her prayers by the heart-rending cry that filled the room. Looking towards Sydney, Katherine watched as Sydney slid to the floor crying, looking like the burden she bore was just too heavy to bear. Quietly Katherine moved from her pew and slid into the pew beside Sydney. Placing her arm around Sydney's shoulders she knelt beside her and looked into the pleading, fear-filled eyes that seemed to beg for some kind of answer. Gathering the crying woman into a hug, Katherine prayed that God would give her the wisdom to answer the questions she knew she was not ready for.

CHAPTER TWENTY

R andy Moorehead was walking towards the chapel to
pray for his friend David, who was still talking with
Pastor Steve. David had so many questions that Randy could
not answer and had been relieved when Steve had offered to
come and talk with him. Randy had been a Christian for only
about a year. He had witnessed the change in Brenda, his
wife, after she had attended a Bible study at Dorothy
Hamilton's home. Dorothy lived just down the street from
the Moorehead's and had always made time to visit with
Brenda and bring meals or baking when they were needed
the most. Brenda worked as a home care worker and some
days she was just too tired to cook. Randy had always been
amazed how Dorothy seemed to know when her help would
be most appreciated. When Dorothy had invited Brenda to
the Bible study at her home, Brenda had gone with some
hesitancy but it was only because of Dorothy that she went.
It wasn't long before the change in Brenda was evident to
Randy and she was able to share the reason for the change.
With all the tragedy that Randy witnessed in his work, the
fact that there was someone who loved him enough to die for
him struck home and Randy knew that he was ready for that

kind of change in his own life.

It had been the most wonderful development and he and Brenda had begun to attend church with Dorothy and her daughter Katherine. Randy now recognized the same restlessness in David that he had experienced before he had given his life over to Jesus Christ. So Randy had been praying for his friend and hoping for an opportunity to talk to him. This accident had really bothered David and when Randy and Steve had gone to talk to him he had a lot of questions. After awhile Randy felt the need to walk and check on the Gillman family. Leaving David talking to Steve, he had sought out the chapel to pray for his friend and the family they had brought in hours earlier. As he had approached the chapel a heart-rending cry had spilled forth into the hallway that had caused Randy's heart to break and he rushed towards the door. Throwing it open, he entered the chapel and stopped short at what he saw. There kneeling in the second pew was Dr. Hamilton with her arms around a crying Mrs. Gillman. Randy knew then that Mrs. Gillman had been the source of the heart-rending cry. Just then Katherine looked up and caught sight of Randy standing in the doorway.

"Randy." Katherine was surprised to see him standing there but then again she thought maybe she shouldn't be. She knew of his commitment to the Lord from her mother and had seen him seek refuge in this very chapel many times during the past year.

"I'm sorry, I heard the cry and thought that someone was in trouble. I will leave you two and find somewhere else pray." Randy started to back out of the room when he remembered something that had slipped his mind earlier.

"Before I leave, there is something I must tell Mrs. Gillman," Randy stopped and walked a little closer towards the two women.

Sydney looked up at Randy with eyes that pleaded for any answer to her questions. "What do you need to tell me?"

Sydney replied and the curtness in her voice took her aback.

"Well, I just remember something that happened in the ambulance when I was bringing your husband to the hospital. I had forgotten it until just now when I saw you. Please forgive me for not telling you sooner, but as I said, I just remembered it." Randy fidgeted and wondered if this was the right time to tell her and if her husband had meant for him to tell her.

"What happened in the ambulance? Did my husband say something? Please tell me." Sydney had come to full attention at what her husband might have said or did that this man remembered. This may be one of the last words spoken by her husband and she needed to know them.

"Well, your husband had a brief moment of consciousness and he said to tell you that no matter what happens that God loves you." Randy had been confused by the words spoken but then again people said some strange things when they were semi-conscious.

"He spoke to you?" Sydney couldn't believe that he had spoken and she was just now finding out about it.

"Yes, but then he slipped back into unconsciousness right after saying that." Randy had thought it strange but at the time he was more concerned with getting him to the hospital than with anything else.

Sydney was struck by the words, "He said to tell me that no matter what happened, that God loves me?" Sydney struggled with the words and what they might mean. Did Grant know that he was going to die? Then why not tell her that he loved her?

"Yes, that is what he said. I will go now and leave you two alone." With that Randy left the chapel and proceeded down the hall to the small waiting room at the end where he could pray. He had the feeling that he should also pray for the two ladies in the chapel as well as David in the cafeteria. Sydney looked at Katherine and asked, "Why would he say that? Why would he be concerned that I know that God loved me?" At the last question a distant memory struck Sydney and she caught her breath.

"What? Is there something that you've remembered?" Katherine had seen the look in Sydney's eyes as though a past memory had been triggered by those words from her husband.

"My . . . my grandmother, the last time I saw her alive she told me to never forget how much she loved me and how much Jesus loved me. Why would Grant say that? I never told him about that. How would he know?" Sydney was not sure what to believe anymore and now she was more confused than ever before. Did this mean that Grant knew that he would never see her again? Panic started to overtake Sydney as she said, "He is going to die. That's what happened to my Grandma Ruth. God is going to take Grant away just like he took my grandmother."

Katherine watched as the panic and fear began to consume Sydney and knew that she had to do something right away to stem this fear. Fear. . .where she had read something about fear today? Katherine knew that she had read something today about fear and love. Now what was it and where had she seen it?

"Sydney, Grant is in surgery and we don't want to jump to any conclusions. I feel very confident that we were able to get him into surgery soon enough. Getting him into surgery and alleviating the pressure in his head as soon as possible will minimize the damage. Sydney, why do you believe that God is going to take Grant away from you?" Katherine continued to try and remember where she had read something about fear but right now she needed to try and get Sydney to focus on something else besides being afraid.

"Because, God took away my Grandma Ruth and then he took away both of my Forrester grandparents in one accident. Now he's going to punish me and take away my husband. Why won't He leave me alone? I have done everything that He wanted and I still don't have enough faith to keep Him from punishing me. He is no God of love and there's just no way that He loves me!" Sydney was overcome with fatigue and knew that she probably shouldn't have unloaded like that on Katherine and yet it felt good to let someone know how she was feeling. She then realized that she had better quit and say no more, especially about the dreams, because Katherine had the authority to have her committed if she decided that Sydney was slowly going crazy. Right now Sydney knew that she had reached a moment of decision. She had to decide to either let the fears consume her and go crazy or to somehow conquer her fears and get on with life. Succumbing to the fears seemed a whole lot more conceivable at this moment than ever conquering them. Maybe she should just give into the fears and quit fighting, for she knew she no longer had the strength to fight. If only Grandma Ruth was here, she always felt safe when she was with Grandma Ruth. It was a safeness that she hadn't felt in a very, very long time.

CHAPTER TWENTY-ONE

Katherine was taken aback by the confession and was unsure how to answer Sydney. This definitely explained the source of the fears that she had seen earlier. Katherine now realized that Sydney's fears were keeping her from seeing how much God truly loved her and from a deeper relationship with Him. The only problem was how to help her realize that her fears were keeping her imprisoned and that her only freedom from them really was in Jesus Christ. Katherine silently prayed, *Lord, please guide me and give me the words that will help Sydney to see how much You truly love her and want to set her free from her fears. Show me Your words and give me Your wisdom.*

Finding strength in her prayer, Katherine slowly slid back on to the pew and helped Sydney as she sat next to her. Scanning the room for some kind of inspiration on how to start, Katherine saw the open Bible on the front table. Love, God's love—that was what she needed to explain to Sydney. That is where she would start.

"Sydney, why would you think that God doesn't love you?" Quietly Katherine turned in the pew to face Sydney while still holding on to her hand.

Knowing that she could not run from this situation and feeling and that it was time to face the fears head on, Sydney opened up and began to share with Katherine.

"When I was ten years old I went to a Bible camp near my hometown of Tilson. I had gone there for a couple of years and it was the thing to do when you went to church. Maria was a counselor there when she was in high school and I thought it was a good way to spend a week away from home. Anyway, the speaker there had there talked about how the angel of the Lord was going to blow the trumpet on the last day and then all of the Christians would go to heaven and those who were not saved would go to hell. Needless to say, it was your basic fire and brimstone sermon. I was scared and wasn't sure whether I was a Christian or not, since I was a good person and I went to church all the time. After the sermon, we where going back to our cabins for devotions and then snacks when someone thought that it would be fun to blow a trumpet to call everyone for snack. I remember there was a lot of crying and kids all over the camp thought that they had been left behind. After things calmed down I asked my counselor to help me pray the prayer that I had heard about in the sermon. When we were done praying, she asked me how I felt and if I felt any different now that I had asked Jesus into my heart." Sydney stopped as she remembered the long ago asked question and how confused she had been by it. Looking down at her hands she continued with her story.

"I told her the truth. I didn't feel any different. She kept asking me if I was sure and that she was sure that I should feel God in me. I was trying to feel Him but I couldn't, so I thought that I must have done it wrong. After camp and the summer I went back to school. Nothing seemed to change for me and I kept trying to feel God. I went to church with my family and did all of the things that I thought good Christians were supposed to do. But there was still nothing.

I spent a lot of time at my Grandma Ruth's house—well, at least as much time as my mother would allow me. I always felt safe when I was there and she made me feel special. I was her Sydney-Bear. It was the day that she gave me my first sip of coffee that was the last time I saw her alive. As I was leaving her house she told me to never forget how much she loved me and how much Jesus loved me. I thought it was strange for her to say that, but as I look back, she must have known that she would never see me again. She was admitted to the hospital and later took her own life."

Sydney closed her eyes at the memory and the tears spilled onto her folded hands. "Why did you leave me? You will never know how much I needed you. Oh Grandma, why did you leave me?"

Katherine watched and waited patiently as Sydney once again grieved the loss of her grandmother. Sensing that she was ready to continue, Katherine gently squeezed her hand in silent encouragement to proceed with the rest of her story.

"I remember getting down on my knees with Maria to pray for my grandmother and that she would come home and be safe. But she wasn't and I knew that God did not answer my prayer because I hadn't been good enough. There was something that I wasn't doing right and that was keeping me from feeling Him. I vowed from that day forward that would live the perfect Christian life and try to make God happy. I did everything—perfect grades, helped with everything I had time for in the church and school, planned and participated in all kinds of youth group activities—everything I could think of. I spent all the time trying to be a good Christian but yet I was hiding my fear that I was not good enough for God and that He was going to punish me again. To be honest, I felt like two different people, the one everyone saw and the one I was hiding. When I had found out that Grandma Ruth committed suicide I feared that I was more like her than I realized and that I was slowly going crazy too. Actually, I feel like I am on the verge of losing my mind and that maybe I should be committed." Sydney looked into the kind eyes of Katherine to see if there was any sign that she also thought that maybe Sydney was crazy. But all she saw there was love and concern. Feeling more comfortable and sensing that Katherine was not ready to have her committed yet, Sydney continued to unload her heart.

"Then I met Grant and I admired how much he loved God and thought that maybe someday I could feel that way too. I never let Grant know about my fear of God and I was very involved in the church. Brendan was only six months old when I received the phone call that my father's parents had been killed by a drunk driver on their way to Sedona. I couldn't believe that God had taken them both away from me at the same time. Now I felt for certain that God did not love me. From that moment, I decided to not follow Him anymore and to just concentrate on my family. For awhile I had bad nightmares about my entire family being killed and that I was the only one left. Many times Grant would wake me from them but I couldn't tell him what they were about. I didn't want him to have to deal with the fact that his wife was going crazy. Soon the dreams subsided and I thought that life would finally be normal for me and that I could put all of this behind me. Then the dreams came back only this time I was at the funeral of all my children and only Grant and I were left of our family. The dreams have become more frequent and last night I had another one. I was being fore-warned about what was going to happen. God was going to punish me again. He is just seeking revenge because I was living my life just fine without Him." Sydney paused. Even now as she was talking out loud and sharing her deepest feelings, she sounded like a woman who needed to be committed. Maybe it was time to admit that she was crazy and just give in to the fears.

Katherine had been silently listening to Sydney and taking it all in. All of her reactions today in the hospital were easily explained now that Katherine knew the history. Her heart broke as she listened to the struggle to please God and her sense of failure. Now was the time for the record to be set straight and for Katherine to share the glorious love of God with Sydney. Feeling a sense of urgency to share with her, Katherine first stopped and prayed for wisdom and guidance in how she shared and for an open and receptive heart in Sydney.

"Sydney, you have shared your heart with me and now I would like to share with you from my own heart. I work in the hospital and I see many tragedies, many much worse than today—where families are not as fortunate as you and take no one home. I have struggled with why God does not stop bad things from happening and why bad people never get hurt and good people die? But one thing I have learned is that we live in a world that is sinful and that people make their own choices, whether good or bad. The most important thing that I have learned is that God loves us more than we could ever imagine and He never leaves us alone in this world." Katherine felt a surge of renewed awe at God's amazing love for her and wanted to make sure that she explained it to Sydney in a way that would leave her feeling the same sense of awe.

"How can you believe that God loves you or me after what I have just told you? Can't you see how He has hurt me over and over?" Sydney couldn't believe that Katherine still believed that God was a God of love.

"Well, I do believe that He loves me and that He loves you. Sydney, your grandmothers loved you because you were their granddaughter, right?'

Hesitating and wondering where this was going to lead, Sydney replied, "Yes."

"Was there anything that you could do to make your

grandmothers love you more?" Katherine looked into Sydney's eyes and saw that fear and confusion still prevailed.

"No, there was nothing I could do to make them love me more; I was their granddaughter and that is why they loved me. What does this have to do with whether God loves me or not?"

"Just one more question and then I will tell you. Was there anything that you could do to make your grandmothers love you any less?" Katherine watched as slowly Sydney realized where the questions were going.

"Not that I know of—like I said, they loved me because I was part of them." Sydney was not sure that she wanted to hear what Katherine was going to say next but she also knew that maybe deep down it was what she wanted to hear.

"Sydney, if your grandmothers loved you simply because you were their granddaughter, then their love was a free gift that you just had to accept, right? All you had to do was accept your grandmothers' free gift of love." Katherine paused and watched as Sydney nodded and looked into her eyes for what she knew was next.

"God loves you because you are His child and there is nothing you can do to make yourself better and there is nothing you can do that will make Him love you less. Sydney, God sent His only Son Jesus down to earth to become a man to live and be tempted just like we are. The only difference is that Jesus never sinned and then He was crucified on the cross as the perfect sacrifice for our sins. After three days, Jesus was raised from the dead and conquered death. He is in heaven at the right hand of God. Sydney, Jesus did this just for you. He loves you and knows everything about you. He doesn't expect you to feel Him— He just wants you to trust that He is there with you all the time. Sydney, God has never left you from the very moment that you asked Him into your heart as a child. He has always heard your prayers, and even though you tried to live a life that you thought was pleasing to Him, all He ever really wanted from you was your love. Sydney, He doesn't want all the things that you do, He wants you." Katherine paused and watched as the realization of all that God wanted was her love flashed in the once fear-filled eyes.

Slowly looking to Katherine, Sydney asked, "Are you sure?"

"Sydney, see that Bible on the front table? Go and read the underlined verses for today." Katherine slid from the pew and let Sydney slowly get up. Hesitantly Sydney walked towards the table and the open Bible. Looking at the open book, she noticed that some verses had been highlighted in yellow. Slowly she read the verses and let the words water her dry and parched soul.

> *We know how much God loves us, and we have put our trust in Him. God is love, and all who live in love live in God, and God lives in them. And as we live in God, our love grows more perfect. So we will not be afraid on the Day of Judgment, but we can face Him with confidence because we are like Christ here in this world. Such love has no fear because perfect love expels fear. If we are afraid it is for fear of judgment and this shows that His love has not been perfected in us. 1 John 4:16-18*

Sydney turned back towards Katherine and whispered, "He knew about my fears and He still loves me? The verse says that His love has no fear and that His perfect love expels fear. Does He really love me that much?"

Katherine rushed to Sydney and took her into her arms and cried, "He loves you even more than that and He has never left you and never will, even when you walk away from Him. All you have to do is reach out and he is always right there."

"Oh Lord Jesus, forgive me for walking away and please help me to realize the depth of your love. Cast all my fears away and fill me with your perfect love." Sydney's heart cried out to the one who loved her and she felt the fears leaving and an overwhelming peace and love fill her heart. Holding on to Katherine, she cried and thanked God for the wonderful gift of His love for now she knew that no matter what happened, God loved her and would never leave her alone. The safeness that she had once known in the presence of her grandmother was now replaced with the safeness of her loving heavenly Fathers presence.

CHAPTER TWENTY-TWO

Three days later Sydney sat at Grant's bedside savoring the words from the book of First John. It had been a very long time since she had read the Bible. She used to think that all it talked about was a God who was vengeful and violent and had no relevance to her life today. But ever since the day in the chapel, Sydney had been reading the Bible with a new sense of awareness to how much the Bible talked about God's love for her. She couldn't believe that she had missed it. Everywhere she turned God's love was revealed to her in a new and awesome way. Anita had given her a concordance to use and she was writing down every verse in the Bible that had the word "love" in it. For two days she had been writing verses and she hadn't even scratched the surface. It was just so amazing to Sydney that she had totally missed God's love and had spent her life dwelling on the fears and letting the fears rule her life.

The fears had tried to resurface when Grant had come out of surgery and the doctor said that all they could do now was wait. She had been scared that he would die or have severe brain damage but then she remembered that God loved her and Grant and that no matter what happened, she would trust Him to get her through. Grant had not regained consciousness yet but she continued to pray that he would and that she would be able to share with him all that God had done for her.

Brendan had come through the surgery and had been relieved to hear that his brother and sister were okay. He was still groggy from the pain medication and when she wasn't at Grant's side, she was with Brendan. Brendan's room was full of cards and flowers from friends and the baseball team, with the latest being delivered by Amanda earlier this afternoon. Sydney had left them alone to visit and had sought out the chair by Grant's bedside in the hope that he would awaken.

Sydney's parents had taken up residence at her home, taking care of Scotty and Sarah Rose. Grant's parents had arrived and taken turns with Sydney sitting by his bedside. Hillary was in after work everyday and was feeling the lack of room in her small basement suite after her other two brothers, Don and Ryan showed up. They were all gone for lunch now and Sydney enjoyed the silence. God had been good by having all the family so close and being willing to take care of things for her so she could be with Grant.

Sydney looked out the window at the sunshine and saw the birds flying in the sky in what looked like a game of tag. She smiled and looked at the pale face of her husband. Reaching up, she slowly caressed the left side of his face. The swelling had gone down some and the bruises were a nasty purple. His leg was in a cast after surgery yesterday to fix the break and he was breathing on his own. For that she was thankful.

As she leaned over the bed to be closer to him she held his hand and closed her eyes. "Lord, thank you for all You have done. Thank you for keeping the children safe and for our families who have come to help. Lord, continue to be with Brendan and heal his wounds. Thank you for all the support and friends that have come to be with him. Lord, thank you for your amazing love and for being here with me. Heal Grant and help him to know how much I love him. Lord, I love you and thank you for loving me." As she finished she felt Grant's hand tighten around hers, and as she opened her eyes, she saw the most wonderful sight in the world. Grant's eyes were focused on her and tears were rolling down his face.

"Grant, oh Grant, you're awake." Sydney could hardly contain herself as she reached up and kissed his face.

"Syd." Grant's voice was weak but he continued, "Syd, are the children okay?"

"Oh Grant, Sarah Rose and Scotty are at home with my parents and Brendan is just down the hall. Oh, Grant you are awake, I can't believe it." Sydney was beside herself with happiness and she didn't know where to start to tell him all that had happened in the last three days.

"Yes honey, I am awake. Now tell me, did I hear you praying?" Grant was hoping that seeing her pray hadn't been a dream.

"Yes, you heard me praying. Grant, thank you for reminding me that God loves me. It has changed my life and I just don't know where to start to tell you all about it." Sydney sat back in her chair and looked into the eyes of the man who had stolen her heart those many years ago at a basketball game. In his eyes she saw love and joy and the tears in her own eyes started to spill over.

"Start from the beginning; I want to hear it all." Grant felt a surge of joy at the thought that his wife had finally found the love of God and he was eager to hear all about it. Watching her and the way her eyes light up as she talked about what God had done in her heart, Grant thought that she was never more beautiful as she was right now. Tears slid down Grant's face as she shared all the fears that she had known and how God's perfect love had conquered her fears.

Sydney had finished telling Grant about everything that had happened and felt like she was closer to him then ever before. Sitting there looking into his eyes, Sydney knew that she had been given her life back. She no longer had to fear God or death because she knew that God loved her and that she would one day see her grandparents again in heaven. God had promised her eternal life and with His love residing in her heart, there was no more room for fear. Sydney knew she had finally found the one true hope that made all of life worth living and that no matter what lay ahead, she could always depend on the unfailing love of God.

Printed in the United States
69087LVS00002B/211-255